GW00686144

mafia!

published in 1993
by the centre for creative and performing arts
university of east anglia, norwich, england

copyright © 1993 by the individual authors
all rights reserved

printed and bound in great britain by
broadgate printers, aylsham, norfolk
typeset in joanna

*all the characters in these stories are fictitious
and any resemblance to actual persons
living or dead, is therefore coincidental*

this book is sold subject to the condition
that it shall not, by way of trade or otherwise
be lent, resold, hired out or otherwise
circulated without the publisher's prior consent
in any form of binding or cover other than that
in which it is published and without
a similar condition being imposed
on any subsequent purchaser

british library cataloguing in publication data
a catalogue record for this book is available from the british library
isbn 0 9515009 4 5

mafia!

an anthology of new fiction
from the university of east anglia's creative writing ma

with an introduction by adam mars-jones

many thanks to:

russell celyn jones, jane chittenden, jon cook,
mike oakes, glenn patterson, phoebe phillips,
anastacia tohill, andy vargo

thanks also to eastern arts association, norfolk
institute for art and design, university of east
anglia computer centre

baby photo courtesy of the
hulton picture company
'handbook of the ark' illustrations by david lewis
'if you have ghosts' written by rocky erickson,
published by orb music/bleib alien saucer
publishing ascap
webster facsimile published by
menton press, england

harriet braun - *editorial*
melanie danburg - *production manager, editorial*
nic laight - *editorial, design*
francis mead - *publicity, production*
derek neale - *editorial*
matthew singh-toor - *design*

contents

introduction

adam mars-jones

ONLY SEX EDUCATION seems to cause more unease in British hearts and minds than the teaching of creative writing. You're going to study *that*? But that's not a subject!

Some of the unease is based on assumptions about education: surely anyone who wants to can write, using tools acquired along the way. This turns out to be largely an assumption about class, and the "anyone" who turns incidentally acquired skills into competent practise would have to be a pretty rarefied creature.

Another unease-factor has to do with gender: a creative writing course sounds suspiciously supportive, amniotic, in a word *unmasculine*. How does authority work in such a setting? Is this like apprenticeship to a craft master? Do you have to make knife-boxes before being allowed to attempt a table?

Creative writing may not be a subject like other

subjects, but it is a quasi-subject, of which I have some experience as both teacher and taught. I have the distinct impression of having benefited as a student (in America in the late '70s), and of having done no harm when I, in turn, became a teacher.

At the same time, as a student I can recall no actual item of advice that turned out to be revelatory or more than dimly helpful, and as a teacher I have no memory of passing on tips that had any sort of value except in the context of a specific piece of prose.

A "course" of creative writing sounds somehow plausible, have you noticed?, while no one would voluntarily refer to a creative writing lesson. The absorption of – what? – is too gradual to be compatible with the sharp outlines and one-way traffic of a "lesson".

The University of Virginia at Charlottesville, when I arrived there in 1978, had a good reputation for English studies and particularly for creative writing. There was an endowment for half-a-dozen writing studentships – the Henry Hoyns Fellowships. (There was also a Benjamin C. Moomaw Award for Oratory and an Emily Clark Balch Prize for a story or poem. The Hoyns, the Moomaw, the Balch: they all sounded like diseases of trees.)

I was supposed to be writing a PhD on American literature, but I never even located the papers in Alderman Library – the Faulkner holdings – which were my excuse for being in the country. Instead I "audited" writing courses – that is, attended classes without getting credit, and without needing to take the deadlines with any great seriousness.

In what turned out to be three years in America, I took writing courses with three tutors all told. The first had a pipe and a latent stutter. His tweediness was neutralised by sportiness – serious distance running in the over-40s category he had just joined. In winter, he would enter the room where the class was held, then dive out again as if he'd forgotten something. He would come back into the room wearing a different woolly cap, and anyone who noticed this, or anyone who spotted the lime-green tennis ball in the fruit bowl at creative writing breakfasts, would receive the standard jocular accolade: *your eye for detail will take you to the top of your profession.* In class he saw his role as comparable to an orchestra conductor's, a matter of balancing forces, and would doggedly defend stories no one else liked.

The second tutor let us know that he was only teaching at all because there was alimony to be paid. He was uncomfortable with the notion of having authority, and didn't want to sit in the conventional teacher's posture, facing the class. This would have been more satisfactory if the chairs in our assigned room hadn't been fixed in place, so that there was no prospect of us creating a supportive circle. Instead out teacher sat behind us all, in the back row. From there his comments, however mild, were inevitably disconcerting – but not as disconcerting as his silence when he withheld comment.

The third teacher was eminent, Southern, gentle-manly. He referred to his post as a sinecure, his reward for a lifetime's literary effort; perhaps it was a mistake to mention this to his students. I assume that's why the contribution I was making to the sine-cure scheme – $387 – is burned on my brain, when nothing else from those years still bears its price tag.

This third tutor's Fall teaching was a conventional class, but his Spring teaching was like a correspon-dence course without the correspondence. He would spend the winter in Key West (he specified "the heterosexual part") until his wife, who remained in Charlottesville to endure the season, was able to promise him that Virginia was once more habitable. On his return, he would spend an individual hour with each student.

Not very much of that hour was, technically, criti-cism. One friend reported that he had divided her stories into two piles. Pointing to one pile, he said, "These stores–" (his Memphis accent suppressed the second syllable of the word) "These stores are good," pointing to the other, "These stores are no good." That – with suave elaboration – was that, for the semester's teaching.

With me he was less definite, perhaps because I had submitted a novella, not so easily divided into two piles. For most of our hour, though, we talked about London, a city he had loved in the past and whose landmarks he was anxious to assure himself were still in place.

A prankster, a weak king afraid of power, and an overcharging absentee. I appreciate that I seem to have sketched a succession of profoundly unhelpful helpers, but that was not how I experienced it. Then again, my project was not learning to write, exactly, but somehow finessing my way to self-belief, when my culture had taught me to prize only diffidence.

I was psychologically much closer to Francis Wyndham, for instance, who after writing a book of short stories in his late teens submitted it to a publisher's, and when it was rejected put his ambitions on hold indefinitely, than I was to William Faulkner – who kept an elaborate chart of which magazine had rejected which story so that he could have the sharp pleasure of resubmitting them, and having them gratefully accepted, once his name was known.

My first teacher, he of the tennis ball in the fruit bowl, was perhaps crucial to my project. His pipe made him a patriarch, but his stutter when it surfaced made him into a shy child. His authority was variable, and if his judgment went against me I would find a way to diminish it definitively.

Just as important, I wasn't taking credits, and could treat deadlines relatively lightly. They were no more than impalpable nudges toward literary production. For this class I wrote my first three stories, "Lantern Lecture" the last of them. This teacher also procured for me (though he made out that these decisions were entirely consultative) that coveted disease of trees a Hoyns Fellowship, which enabled me to stay in the States for another year.

If the other people in the class had sincerely disliked my stuff, I could always have told myself that they were after all *Americans*, not attuned to the nuances in which I so thrillingly dealt. But in fact adverse criticism is not necessarily as threatening as misplaced enthusiasm. To be praised for something you didn't intend, something in fact you set out to avoid, is a truer rite of passage for a writer. Thereafter you must imagine the relationship between reader and writer differently.

By the time I encountered my second teacher, he who sat behind us, I was sufficiently confident to think, not *I don't understand this method*, but *What a daft way to go about it*. Even so, the course was not a dead loss. Our teacher happened also to teach a course on Law and Literature in Nineteenth Century America, and his references to this subject irritated me into writing a novella which assumed that law and literature, in the teeth of his line of argument, were profoundly incompatible ways of looking at the world. To him, in a sense, though he read only fragments of it, I owe "Bathpool Park".

Even the third teacher, the winterer in Key West's respectable quarter, did no harm, since I realised I too could travel (writing classes were my only actual commitment), and spent Mardi Gras 1980 in New Orleans with a clear conscience.

From the University of Virginia's Creative Writing Program I was able to derive not only confidence and a regular incitement to produce fiction, but the money that translates into time. When I returned to Britain, I had a full-length manuscript to my credit, however little I expected it would be published.

It may be, in fact, that all of these things – confidence, mild peer pressure, money as time – are more important than an actual teacher. Certainly groups with a shared agenda – women's groups, or gay groups like the Lavender Quill Club in New York round 1980 – can manage quite well without.

But some sort of structure is most often necessary, and if there were more courses like the University of East Anglia's in this country, the hostility and embarrassment that surround the subject would – surely? – soon die away.

What's the worst thing that can be said about sex education classes? That they only tell you what you already know, or else that they put you off the whole business altogether. The objections to writing classes are no more substantial. Why shouldn't people explore their natural curiosity about where stories come from?

casper

harriet braun

harriet braun was born in london in 1968. she studied drama and film studies at bristol university. she was the first person to recieve the curtis brown scholarship for study on the m.a. in creative writing.

THE TRUNK arrived today. It's perfect, C.C.F.T. embossed on the front in gold. A little ostentatious, I know, but Casper will be pleased. He probably won't show it of course; he's so spoilt. He'll just say something like, "Yes, very good, Smithers, put it by the window," throw a glance at it and carry on reading. But he has to be allowed his arrogance. It becomes someone of his station. It simply wouldn't do to have him fawning over a trunk now, would it? Casper is destined for great things.

I'm very pleased with the trunk, but there's a long way to go till we're ready for school. It's so exciting. I'm really starting to see the possibilities. I run my hand across the lettering: Casper Cuthbert Fotherington Thomas. I still don't know if I'm entirely satisfied with the surname; it may be a little clichéd, but I had to make a decision. I was getting impatient. I ponder for a while, then get so excited that I take off all my clothes and lie across the trunk in a manner befitting Casper, one arm lazily propping up my head. I need the other free, obviously. "Leave it over there, Smithers," I say, as I'm about to come. At orgasm I despair over the declining standard of servants.

The hair isn't right. What beautiful hair, such a pretty little girl, people used to say. I remembered that and in my arrogance hung onto it. Fair hair down to my shoulders. It's also been useful in attracting the right types. Some very butch women still gravitate towards the merest hint of femme. But I'm bored with that. It's so hard to keep a casual encounter... casual. "Will I see you again? Can I have your phone number?" Very irritating.

There was one woman who had possibilities. "What do you fantasize about? What turns you on?" she said. I realised that my distraction during our brief sexual encounters must have been evident, but at least she had the guts to ask. I thought about it for a moment, mulled it over. "Oh I don't know," I said eventually, in a manner which indicated that the conversation was closed. The fact of the matter was, when faced with the opportunity of articulating my needs, I'd realised that I didn't know what they were. I only knew they weren't being met.

That was date four. On date five she said, "I think I'm falling in love with you." I nearly choked. There was no date six. I haven't been close to anyone for years, it's a little late to start now.

But I'm grateful to her. She was the catalyst. The

very direct nature of her question forced me to look at myself and, in doing that, I made my find. It wasn't the first time that I'd been concerned by my relation to things sexual. Lust has always been something to be satisfied quickly; someone catching my eye, a flicker of interest, a fuck. Urgent, fast, and once over, nothing, save for boredom, and a sense of frustration. A desire for something more, something else.

What do I fantasize about? Now there was a thought. Not a great deal really, but maybe, just maybe... I set myself something of a project, a quest to find the desirable. Initially there was the usual mundane and uninspired array of genitalia floating across my mental landscape. But that didn't answer my question. So for a few days I tried new images, anything I thought might turn me on. It was like browsing through a book shop hoping to hit upon a good read. Nothing, until one day a brief image that aroused such an overwhelming feeling of the illicit, I was overcome. It wasn't something new, but something old, very old.

I was eleven, in the cinema, drawn into a world that bore no similarity to my own, save for one thing. In this depiction of public school and cricket matches, dorms, fags, chums, and aristocracy, something went on that struck a chord. Something that inspired the same warm feeling I got when hiding in my sister's cupboard watching her undress, or stealing furtive glances at my schoolfriends in the changing rooms after netball. In this film, boys fell in love with boys. I'd discovered I was not alone. I used my pocket money to go back to the cinema again and again until the film was no longer playing. Yet its departure didn't quell my desire to climb into the screen and join in.

It didn't stop there either. I was soon to discover that there was more. One day in my uncle's house I came across a book. It was lying face-down by the side of his bed; the words 'homosexual love' on the back-cover. I'd heard my mother use this phrase in hushed tones to my Aunty Ellen. I wasn't entirely sure of its meaning, but I knew it made me feel guilty. I'd ease off on hiding in my sister's cupboard, and try to stop imagining what the women in *Little House on The Prairie* looked like with no clothes on.

The book that I'd come across was *Maurice*. On first finding it I only allowed myself the briefest glance. I felt that if I was even caught in close proximity to the word homosexual it was enough to secure my immediate disgrace. On going home I became completely preoccupied with it. The book, like the film before it, filled my thoughts. On my frequent visits with my mother to Uncle John I took to sneaking away and taking the book off the bookshelf. Then, with heart pounding and sweaty palms, I'd leaf through, looking for... I didn't know quite what. The sensation this inspired was, at the same time as being terribly frightening, almost unbearably sexy. It was on one of these occasions that I found the reference to the unspeakable act of the Greeks. Horrified, the full import of my illicit activities occurred to me. I realised that I might be an unspeakable.

Had my Uncle John been an Aunty Joanna, and the book *The Well of Loneliness* and not *Maurice*, well, who knows? As it was, to my knowledge, I was the only unspeakable female ever. In order to be able to indulge in unspeakable activity, I needed to be a boy, preferably aristocratic and attending public school. I was in something of a quandary. Now, fourteen years later, a long buried quandary had re-surfaced.

I've been sleeping with women for a number of years, but when the point came that I could acknowledge my unspeakability to myself and others, it was a little late. I hadn't fumbled at parties, forged juvenile relationships: things I'd once heard described as 'practising for marriage'. If you've stood outside the window for long enough, it's silly to imagine that on stepping in you will no longer feel cold. I can only ever see intimacy, after the initial lust has been satisfied, as a clawing intrusion; embarrassing, unnatural almost. Until now that is, until the emergence of Casper.

Casper is getting his hair cut today. He's been in existence for a few weeks. I've hardly been able to wait to get home from work in order to play around with my new found friend. As with anything though, excitement can be short lived. I need pastures new.

It's not enough to crawl into bed at night to thoughts of dormitories and illicit meetings in the games cupboard, delectable though those things are. Casper wants to walk and talk. Casper wants to wander around my bedroom. Casper wants to own things, and now Casper has his very own school trunk with a tuck box inside it. As yet though he has no haircut and no clothes to speak of. Casper the nudist just won't do! Although he does have a lot of fun with his trunk. He finds it very exciting to get up in the middle of the night and indulge in a naughty piece of tuck. So exciting that sometimes Casper sneaks back for another packet of Rolos, at great danger to himself. Casper's housemaster is very stern and doles out beatings like smarties.

It has not escaped my notice what a good time Casper could have getting his hair cut, yet this poses something of a problem. You see, ordinarily I'd go to a hairdresser, but that simply won't do for a public school boy. I've spotted a barber just down the road. I've walked past it a few times but have been too scared to go in. It's not the loss of my hair that bothers me any more—in fact I positively relish the prospect—it's the questions that might be asked. What am I doing getting my flowing tresses cut off in a barber? Will the barber not find this a little odd?

Yes, that's right, I say, I'm in a play. I'm playing the part of a boy in a play and I'd like an Eton crop. Casper is going to have a hair cut to match his school. Only the very best of schools for Casper. The barber chats about the amateur dramatic production of *My Fair Lady* that he's in. I'm bored, but I don't show it. Casper is far, far more vicious than me. Oh, the damned proletariat, thinks Casper. Why, oh why do I have to suffer this bumbling idiot? I'm shocked; I'd never think such a thing, but at the same time Casper's naughtiness, his blatant snobbery, is ever so arousing. I think about exactly what Casper would do in this situation, as I stare into the mirror, watching the hair fall away from my face. I know that Casper doesn't suffer fools lightly. Casper would bury his face in a book, after having given the barber a disdainful look. I get wet simply thinking about it.

Clutching my play excuse close to my chest, I leave the barber and head for Keats, the school uniform store. I'm on a roll and don't want to lose the impetus. I feed the same line to the shop assistant and, unfortunately, she finds the whole idea most intriguing. How much money do I have in my budget? What's the play? When's it on? Can she come and see it? I hadn't really anticipated any of this. I tell her not to worry about the expense and am as evasive as possible about the rest. I'm surprisingly offhand and bossy as she brings me different variations of school uniform to try on. Is it possible that this is Casper being a naughty boy again? He's really coming into his own these days.

When she goes to see to another customer I stand and assess myself in the dressing room mirror. My hair now flops lazily over one eye. I run my hand across the unfamiliar texture of the short bristles on the back of my neck. I'm sporting the items Casper has settled on: black slacks, a black blazer, a white shirt open at the collar, no tie. The lack of tie is an indication of his rascal devil-may-care attitude to life. Fortunately, I'm skinny, with no chest to speak of. Casper looks in the mirror and likes what he sees. He's an arrogant little so and so, but I grow fonder of him by the minute.

He rests his head against the wall and stares at himself; a petulant look comes across his face. I know what's bothering Casper. He's had a tiff with his new found friend, Ted. He's pained. He shuts his eyes and thinks about Ted. Then he opens his eyes and looks at himself thinking about Ted. Yes, a dashingly tragic figure, he thinks. The love that Casper and Ted share is so pure, so sweet. Something he's aware he could never achieve with a woman. He thinks about yesterday evening when they punted down the river. Talked about how nice England is and how tea is the best drink, walked across daffodil filled, moonlit fields and other such romantic-poet-type activities. He's filled with longing. Oh Ted! he thinks. No, maybe, Oh Edward! No, definitely Ted; it has a better ring to it. I leave the dressing rooms a few minutes later and purchase the items. I've never wanked in a shop before.

By the time Casper and I get home he's also the

proud owner of cricket whites, bat and ball. He rushes over to his trunk and packs them away neatly, then, almost immediately, gets them out again and puts them on. I stare at Casper in the mirror. He really is a fine figure of a man. He knocks a few mock shots into the mirror. "I say, chaps," he calls out to his friends, "fancy a knock-about in the nets?" Then he hits the ball around the room a bit, like the boisterous young scally-wag he can be at times. He does this until the people downstairs start banging on the ceiling. Oh, how damned tedious this life is, he thinks as he flops down on the bed and daydreams about Ted.

Casper is becoming demanding, taking up more and more time. Casper thinks it's tedious that I have to go to work. He wants to stay in and compose love sonnets to Ted. He's rather proud of his poetry, particularly yesterday's effort, which, it has to be said, moved him more than a little:

Oh Ted.
How I love your head, Ted
and Ted, isn't tea the best drink?
Don't you think?
Ted.

So of late I've been indulging him a little and phoning in sick. I've developed a mysterious and prolonged stomach complaint. It's the kind of thing that I can imagine Casper having. He's a delicate sort, the refined type. Too delicate almost for this world, so he's choosing to live in it less and less, which suits me fine. He's feeling particularly bad of late, for a very good reason. Yesterday he had a run in with his friend Perkins. Their relationship has always been turbulent. Perkins thinks Casper is a bit of a rotter and has no time for what he terms his 'self indulgent melancholia.' Perkins fails to notice Casper's inner fragility.

The run-in was in my bedroom. Casper was leaning nonchalantly against the window staring into the middle distance. He looked dashing, if I might say so myself. It's something about the way the light catches his hair, frames the fine line of his jaw. He does this often, especially when fretting over one of his many rows with Ted. It was his morbid attitude that prompted Perkins to tell him off.

"I say, old chap," he said. "Why don't you get a grip. You'll be leaving school soon and putting all these silly crushes behind you." As you can imagine, Casper was absolutely beside himself. How wrong could Perkins be? Their love, a silly crush!

"What rot! Don't you understand, old man," he said. "I'm never going to love women, never!" Casper and I are aware of the irony, but we try to ignore it. In fact, this is a favourite moment of ours which we return to again and again. I have now incorporated a cigarette which Casper can drag on moodily. It makes him all the more petulant and loveable.

I've realised, of late, that although Casper and I are

having a good time, he would benefit from some company. I've never felt more myself than when I'm with Casper, or happier, but I can't help wondering if there's someone else out there, someone just like him. It's time for Casper to meet the outside world. Casper wants to act on this idea straight away. But how exactly?

Casper has a plan. He's searching through the personals in a gay magazine, looking for inspiration. Exactly how to introduce himself? It's a dilemma I'm familiar with: having wandered around for years, scavenging for clues, looking for ways in which to recognize myself, I'm nothing if not diverse.

Eventually Casper picks up a pen and writes:

Lesbian boy seeks chums for public school fun.

violin lessons

derek neale

derek neale was born in birmingham in 1957 and gained an honours degree in english and drama from the university of east anglia in 1990. in the interim he travelled and worked in europe and canada, and lived in northumberland, north yorkshire, and north wales. he now lives in norwich and is working on his first novel.

1

"WHAT do you think you're doing?" I say. He just stands there leaning over the split door; doesn't run away, doesn't say anything. Kids are always snooping around, coming down the lane on their way to the woods. They run off when they see me. They look at me as if I'd eat them alive. This one's wearing his school uniform. Eleven, I'd say, twelve at the outside; his green and black tie flapping in the wind. I press the red button and the lump of oak on the lathe whirs and slows. Still on the threshold, I'll say that for him; waiting until he's invited.

I go over and unlatch the bottom half of the door: the workshop used to be a stable, I keep the top half open to let a bit of air in. There's a lot of dust in this job. It kills your sense of smell. I look at him, trying to catch his eye. He looks in a way that makes me wonder, makes me think I'm not there. He looks everywhere but at me.

"What do you do in here?" he says. His voice echoes around the rafters. It's not often I get a visitor; not here, not in the workshop.

"Come in, if you like. Have a look." I say, "Have to take that tie off though." If there's a rule worth having it's that one: no loose clothing of any description. "Before you know it the circular saw will have it," I tell him. "Or else it'll get wrapped around the lathe. And you'll go with it."

I let him press the green button; click and whir, the oak starts to spin. He wants to see me in action. I tell him not to sit on the mahogany; it's still seasoning and might warp. He stands and watches.

"What's it going to be?" he says.

"A chair leg," I tell him. "My speciality legs." I point to the pile I've done that week. He picks one up and says it looks like a pillar:

"My sister's old dolls' house has got pillars just like that."

"Then your sister's a lucky girl," I say. I don't believe him. Dolls' houses don't have proper pillars. My legs have all the right proportions; Ionic chair legs of the classic order, fluting and all. The only thing I add are the carvings in the capital.

"Keeps her love letters in there now. And her French letters."

"What?" I say. I don't know what he's talking about.

"In the dolls' house, doesn't think I know. What do

you expect from a girl!" I reach for the half inch chisel and tell him not to rest his foot on the mahogany.

"I'm going to make an electric guitar when I'm in the fourth year."

I pretend not to hear him. "Shouldn't you be at home?" I say.

"I'm waiting for my sister."

"And where's your sister?"

"Violin lesson, down the lane with Mr. Bouillon. I'm supposed to sit and listen to that racket! I usually go down the woods."

He searches in his pockets, pulling out his rolled up tie. It unravels like an escaped snake onto the floor. He looks at me and picks it up before I can say anything, but I'm thinking of the dream; the violin and the woods. I dreamt it again last night:

I'm walking in the woods, but there are no leaves crackling under foot, no birds singing or branches creaking. Not a whisper. There's a man standing under a silver birch, playing a violin as if his life depended on it. I don't see his face but I feel as if I know him. He seems possessed by the music but I can't hear it. I strain, I stop breathing, but I can't hear it. I have this dream regularly. I wake up happy, like I've been on a long journey. I've come to think there is no music. Only a picture, that's all.

I press the red button, staring at the mahogany; a ball of green and black springing to life, rolling off the wood into the shavings on the floor. I realise it's the boy's tie. I look down and see him staring at me defiantly, dangling something wrinkled and wet in the air between us.

"Want a French letter?" he says. "I found it in the woods. Hasn't been used."

He pushes it towards my face and I tell him to go.

2

Mr. Bouillon walks past the door. He nods and smiles. My mouth is full of cheese sandwich; some of it falls out as I try to smile back. He's about my age, young for a violin teacher. They say he lives alone but once I saw him walking down the lane with a young woman. She had ginger hair. I made him a set of rush chairs last year. They were in ash, simple things; he didn't want any carving on them. I throw the rest of my sandwich out for the birds and watch Mr. Bouillon walking under the ash tree at the edge of the woods. He usually goes for a walk about this time.

I prefer mornings. In the morning the woods are empty, save for the blackbirds and thrushes rustling in the undergrowth. I could go to work in the van, drive round, but I like to walk. It's a habit of mine; I like kicking through the dew, breaking the spiders' webs across the path. I always stick to the path, but my eyes wander through the mist rising over the pond, up to the glowing red pine bark, and down through the dappled grey lines of beech. I get my ideas there, for the carvings. I gather the shapes like kindling; twigs of light, branches of shadow. I bring it all back here and then I set to work; drawing, measuring, planning. That's where all the hard work's done, the construction. Shapes and ideas are nothing without hard work, and a solid framework. It's table legs this month; Doric. They have to be sturdier, less ornate: but the bevel in the shaft presents a challenge. One slip either way and I've had it.

*

The boy lets himself in and goes straight over to the circular saw. He touches the still blade with his finger tips.

"Dad doesn't think Mr. Bouillon's a very good teacher," he says. "He's going to send her somewhere else."

The boy comes every Wednesday now, while his sister has her violin lesson. He says he wants to be my apprentice, but he's got a long way to go. He does some sanding and a little hand sawing. Most of the time he stands watching; making me think out loud, asking what wood I'm using, and nagging me to split some plinths on the circular saw. That's his favourite; watching it slice through, straight as a die. Sometimes he sits on the mahogany and I tell him to get off. He laughs about it but he gets up.

I look up and see the boy's hand is still on the blade.

"Get your hand off that saw!" I say. He gets a comb from his pocket. Using the saw blade as a mirror he combs his hair.

"Why are all your legs like pillars?" he says. "Why don't they ever have curves in them?"

"They do have curves," I say. "Of course they have curves." But the boy has put his comb away and is swaying backwards and forwards, outlining a figure of eight with his hands:

"A bit of... you know."

I don't know what he means but something is nagging; at the back of my head, something to do with the legs. The man in the dream flashes through my mind. I know there's a curve in the picture, the sort of curve the boy's talking about, but I can't make it out. I can't remember.

The boy is staring at me. I'm hot and sticky. I pull at his tie and he says "okay". He unties the knot slowly and slides it off. He stuffs it in his pocket without rolling it.

"How do you do this?" he says. I have to think for a moment.

"Well," I say, "first of all you decide on materials, which wood and what size. Then there's the shape and style to consider."

"No," he says, "I mean, why do you do it?"

"Why? Because I get satisfaction from it, of course,

from getting a lump of rough old wood and seeing it grow into something new, something that I've..."

"Carved up," he interrupts. "That's what you do isn't it? Just carve it up." My mouth is dry, I can't talk. I look around at the table legs stacked against the wall, and the table tops and cross-members next to them. I feel trapped. I want to put all the parts together, to stack them up and burn them.

The boy sits on the mahogany picking his nose. I tell myself it's almost over. A few more Doric legs and it will all be done. That's what I always tell myself: I just pick a new job, a new horizon, and aim for it. It doesn't matter how difficult it is, doesn't matter if it never gets made. But I've got to have the next job somewhere, I've got to be thinking about it. I wave my chisel at the boy but he doesn't get up off the mahogany. He's not looking. He's scowling over towards the door. I turn and see a white blouse and a mass of ginger hair. I can't see a face.

"Who's that?" I say, before I can stop myself.

"Verruca with the big bazookas," says the boy.

"Veronica, if you don't mind," she says. "I've come to get my baby brother."

She raises her head and sweeps her hair back. I don't understand. I thought his sister would be younger. She looks too old for a school uniform, too old for violin lessons. She looks down at her tie; she's trying to put it on but hasn't fastened the top buttons of her blouse.

"Can I come in?" she says.

"You'll have to take that off," says the boy, pointing over to the tie.

"Why?" she says, guarding the unfastened part of her blouse with her hands. She looks at me as if I might hurt her.

"Safety," I say, trying to sound reassuring. "Machine tools you see. I make it a general rule, no loose fitting clothing."

"You heard him," says the boy. "Get 'em off."

I turn back to the lathe and pretend to look for another chisel.

"Shut up you..." she says but I press the green button. The lathe starts whirring and I can't hear what they shout at each other, only the tone of their voices. I feel as though I shouldn't be there. The pine leg spins faster and my chisel cuts deep, ringing the wood below the capital. This one's almost finished, spinning on its side like a fallen ballerina. I think of new shapes, of curves and twists; the next job. But I don't know what it is.

I press the red button. While the leg slows and stops I put the chisels away. The boy sits on the mahogany, sorting through his pockets. I look at him and feel helpless. His sister has let herself in. She leaves her violin by the door and wanders around touching things. She holds her tie by her side and leans over the pine leg on the lathe, sniffing at the uncut wood on the bench.

"Beautiful smell," she says. "What is it?"

"Damson," I say. "Does it smell nice?"

"Can't you smell it?" She picks it up and holds it up to my nose. I can smell nothing. She puts the wood back on the bench and leans over it again:

"Mm... you don't know what you're missing."

My stomach's rolling and I feel hot. I'm looking at her. She's holding her hair back. A silver cross, a crucifix on a chain, hangs out of her blouse. It dangles onto the lathe. In my mind the lathe starts turning and I want to tear the chain from her neck. I look at the green and red buttons, start and stop, side by side, then back at the crucifix; the face, and the thorns sticking into the head. I imagine the blood, the weight of the body, sagging. I feel my lips curl but I don't know why I'm smiling.

She looks up and sees me staring. She smiles but seems uneasy. Her hand snatches at her blouse and she fastens the buttons up to the neck. She glances over at the boy then smiles at me in a different way. She's sure of herself now.

"Could you teach me how to use this?" she says, putting her hand on the lathe.

"Veronica!" says the boy.

"I'd really like to learn. Why not?"

I don't know what to say, but she doesn't seem to expect me to say anything. She puts her foot up on the bench, smoothing down her black tights. She pulls at the lace of her shoe.

"I'm going," says the boy. He gets up but waits at the door. She ties her lace slowly. I feel angry, I want to get back to work. I pick up a chisel, but her leg is too close; I can't reach the green button. I don't try. I think she's going to tie her other shoe lace but she wanders off round the mahogany to the door. She smiles at me when she picks up her violin, but she's smiling through me, as if I'm not there. The boy looks at her as though he hates her and walks off. I hear her shout down the lane; "What's the matter with you?" I press the green button and see a school tie, curled out on the mahogany.

3

It's Wednesday but I don't expect the boy to come. He hasn't been for three weeks now, not since his sister saw me staring at her crucifix. But the boy's tie has helped me with the next job. It lies on the mahogany, a green and black snake, curling and swerving, slinking round. Twisting. It's alive. The mahogany's beginning to warp but I'm not too worried; I don't think I'll be needing it. I'm ordering the new wood tomorrow.

I'm drawing curves. It's a new experience for me, I've no means of measuring them. It's the next job, the early stages. I wrecked the bevel on two legs this morning; it was no use carrying on. I kept going too far, cutting too deep or using the wrong chisel. I wasn't myself; I kept thinking about the crucifix, that and the dream. The dream has changed. There's usually a storm now. I stand in the woods, the branches whipping all around me. The rain pours into my eyes so I can't see, but I feel as if the man's still there, playing his violin. I want more than ever to hear the music, I want him to be playing one of those hymns; 'To be a Pilgrim', or 'Onward Christian Soldier Marching as to War'. Sometimes I hear a screech, like violin strings being scratched and stretched. Most of the time all I can hear is the wind whipping the branches. I try to look, but the rain drives into my eyes so I have to turn away.

*

The boy reaches over and unlatches the bottom half of the door. He lets himself in. He looks different, he's unsure; he's wearing jeans and a sweater. I offer him one of my cheese sandwiches. He stands, stiff as a board, not wanting to look me in the eye.

"Have you seen Veronica?" he says.

"No, I haven't," I say. But I feel strangely guilty, as if I'm lying. I think of the crucifix dangling over the lathe.

"She's gone missing," he says. "She went to her new violin class on Monday. No one's seen her since."

I feel clumsy, I don't know what to say. I look at the

tie, curled up on the mahogany. Before I can stop my-self I tell him: "You left your tie." He picks it up and examines it.

"It's not mine," he says, and looks up at me. The tie hangs from his hand down to the ground, the curves all straightened out. I wish I hadn't mentioned it.

"It's hers," he says. He's looking hard into my eyes, searching but drawing back at the same time, as if he's scared, as if I might eat him alive.

"Sh... She must have left it," I stutter, "last time you were here." His eyes scan from one side of my face to the other, looking for something, looking as if he might run at any moment.

"Has she been here?" he says.

"No," I say. "Not since that last time, the last time you were here."

He still looks at me but he's not searching anymore, at least I don't think so. I wait to make sure but the silence is more than I can bear. "Your mother and father must be worried," I say, but I realise straight away that they must be more than worried. Much more. I cover my mouth with my hand. I don't know why I'm smiling, I know that it's wrong. He looks up to the rafters, and I see he's grabbing at something, something that he's heard.

"She was going to go to college next year," he says. Did he hear his parents say it? Did he hear their voices crack? His voice doesn't crack. It's just serious. He looks at me as if I know something.

4

When I drove past Mr. Bouillon's house this morning
I saw them putting up a For Sale sign just inside the
gate. They say he's already gone. I wonder whether he
took the rush chairs with him. I drive round in the van
every morning now. After the boy came and told me
about his sister I started seeing faces everywhere;
hanging in the honeysuckle, nestling in the branches,
even in the mud around the pond. The faces were all
smiling; her smile. They stayed with me even when I
got here. I shut the door, top and bottom, trying to
keep them out. But they kept coming and I kept seeing the crucifix dangling over the lathe as it span
round, thorns wrapped around the pale white wood,
blood splashing everywhere. It's just as well I managed to finish the table legs when I did.

It put a bit of a shadow over things. But I won't be
needing the lathe or the circular saw half as much
with the new job. I picked up a bending iron yesterday, now all I've got to do is teach myself how to use
it. I made the moulds out of some beech that I've had
for years, it's well seasoned. I decided on a Guarnerius, it seems the easiest to start with. I'm picking
up the wood this afternoon, after I've been to the
record library.

I stopped having the dream. Well, I stopped

remembering it. I still wake up some days with the same feeling, as if I've been on a long journey. I still want to hear the music. That's why I joined the record library. Beethoven's my favourite, the violin concerto. It's the sort of music that stays with you, keeps you going.

*

I feel a tap on my back as I'm bending into the van to get the last piece of sycamore.

"What have you got there?" says the boy, but he walks off into the workshop before I can tell him. He sits down on the mahogany, leaning forward, with his elbows on his knees. His tie hangs in a straight green and black line, down to the floor.

"What is it?" he says, as I bring the last load in.

"Well," I say, "this is sycamore for the back, ribs, head and neck. And this is Swiss pine for the belly." I pick up a piece of each to show him: I want to show him how pleased I am with it.

"What are you making, a body?" he says. "What's this?" He jumps up and grabs the ebony from the dust sheet covering the circular saw: "Bloody hell, it's like lead." I start to explain but he puts it down on the mahogany and peeps under the sheet covering the lathe. "What happened to your legs?" he says. "I liked your legs." I pick up the ebony and take it over to the bench, out of his reach. I feel as if I should guard it.

"Well, what happened to the legs?" he says. My fingers stroke the smooth black surface of the wood, and I remember her tying her shoelace, her foot up on the bench where the ebony sits.

"I've got a new job on now," I say, trying to pull myself out of it. But I've started thinking: the crucifix dangling down over the lathe.

"Suppose you want me to take this off," he says, starting to undo his tie.

"No," I say. "There's no need." He's not listening and takes it off anyway. He puts his feet up on the mahogany, so he's almost lying down. He looks at me as if he wants me to say something.

"It's alright," I say. "You can sit on there now. I've got no use for it."

He stretches out, looking at me all the time, as if he's waiting for me to say something else. But I'm watching the tie. It's alive; green and black, next to him on the mahogany, curled out and twisting.

"What about..." I say, but he gets up slowly from the mahogany and walks away. "No," I say, "What about the... What about your sister?" I feel guilty about asking.

"Her?" he says, his voice rising as if he's just smelt something rotten. He looks like he doesn't want to talk about it. I don't understand. I see the crucifix catching on the lathe and pulling her down, the chain cutting into her neck, pulling her down.

"But what happened?" I say, I can't help myself.

"What happened?"

"She's in Brighton," he mumbles, "with Mr. Bubblegum."

"What?"

"Mr. Bouillon, the violin teacher," he says. "Ran off with him. What a slut!"

"I thought..." but I don't know anymore what I thought.

"She rang," he says, "but not before half the country was out looking for her. Dad went berserk. He's going down there next weekend to try and find them."

I think of his sister and Mr. Bouillon round a table drinking tea, sitting on rush seats. My chairs in Brighton, by the sea. The boy looks up and asks me what I'm smiling about. He kneels down, picking up the moulds from the floor: "What are these?"

"The next job," I say. "Moulds for the next job." I can't stop smiling, I want to tell him.

"Violins?" he says, his voice cracking. "What do you want to make violins for?"

I tell him I'm going to start with a Guarnerius, just to see how it goes; I'll work my way up to a Stradivarius. Then I might even try the odd viola or even a cello, who knows. But violins will be my mainstay, violins are what I want to make. I rush to the shelves at the back of the workshop, to get the drawings to show him, but as I'm coming back with them the boy drops the moulds down onto the mahogany. They bounce off onto the floor and I run over to pick them up.

"You stupid boy!" I shout, "Be careful with them!" And I brush the shavings off them, shouting at him all the time, "You stupid, stupid boy!" They're not broken but I'm still shouting at him, I can't stop. He turns to the door and grabs his tie, looking up at me as if I'm in the rafters, his eyes wide, as if I fill the whole workshop.

I watch him run down the lane. I'm not shouting now, just staring off into the branches of the ash tree on the edge of the woods. The wind curls the leaves silver-side up, and I think of the rush chairs tucked under the table, down there in Brighton. It makes me think; I wonder if his sister and Mr. Bouillon... I want to call out to the boy and stop him but he's already passed the ash tree. I think of the rush seats, down there by the sea, and I see two violins resting on them.

Two new Guarnerius.

the saint on the landing

joanne reardon

joanne reardon was born in liverpool and lives in oxford, where she is the literature development worker for oxfordshire. since graduating from leicester university in 1983, she has worked in marketing and public relations, completing an mba in 1986. her work has been performed on bbc radio 4.

IT WAS generally agreed that my cousin Lottie told the best stories. They were always fantastic, usually funny and sometimes true.

Every year we were taken to the south coast of Ireland to stay with Nana Mary who lived in a large grey tenement house on the edge of Cork. There were four of us: me, my younger brother Sam, Lottie, and her sister Alice. We sat in the back of the yellow Mini with Mum and Aunty Maeve in front. I always had to sit in the glove pocket, a cushion stuck under my bum for comfort. Alice, who was the eldest, got the other pocket, and Lottie and Sam got the best seat in the middle. Lottie said it was on account of her feeling sick if she couldn't see straight ahead of her. Sam was the smallest so that made sense, but Alice had the longest legs and sat stuffed in her corner uncomplaining. That was how Alice was, and what Alice didn't complain about was made up for by Lottie.

It took hours to drive from the blackened Dublin

dockyard to Nana's cosy house packed full of curios, hidden cupboards, and a saint on every landing.

The pattern of arrival was the same each year. In a rush of voices and unfamiliar accents, mixed with hugs and kisses and haven't-they-growns, we made straight for the big round kitchen table with its steaming brown pot of tea and places set with butter knives of different rainbow-coloured handles. We had cakes and sandwiches washed down with gossip, and as soon as she had overcome her initial reserve Lottie insisted on making conversation with Uncle Joe, my grandfather's brother. He divided his time between the kitchen hob and a copy of the Irish Times, in which he would study the form for races he never saw.

There were so many relatives coming and going throughout those summer weeks, so many who were important in our everyday lives. I never see any of them now.

Uncle Ted was our favourite, never tiring of our chatter, encouraging the endless plans and games we devised for ourselves. He told us stories about Barney the Bull and the fairies on the riverbank, and even promised us that we might meet a leprechaun or two. He was always around, but I was never quite sure where he fitted in.

Uncle Ted took us out on 'picnic days' to all the places Mum and Aunty Maeve had seen a hundred times before. By the time I was ten I think we'd seen every ancient monument and castle in the West of

Ireland. The only place we'd never been was Kinsale, where, we were told, ghosts walked, battles had been fought, and strange fish from the Atlantic could be bought and bartered on the quayside at sunset. Every day during that last holiday in Ireland we waited for Uncle Ted to take us to Kinsale. Finally, on a thundery day in August, Aunty Maeve told us over breakfast that Uncle Ted would come to collect us at two. We were to be ready to go immediately after lunch as it would take an hour to get there, leaving us the morning to kill.

The smell of pigs' trotters steaming on the stove drove us from the kitchen. Lottie said they were the devil's feet and Sam ran to tell Nana who pushed us into the front room with a box of crayons and a wad of paper. Uncle Joe was sitting behind his newspaper, next to the gas fire warming his feet. None of us took any notice of him as we settled down to a reluctant morning's drawing and, even more reluctantly, to Lottie's singing. This didn't last long. Alice, much to our relief, sent Lottie out to the penny shop to buy a selection of sweets which she was to bring back to share with us. Alice, who always gave her sister the benefit of the doubt, had more faith in her completion of this task than I did. Half an hour later, in rushed a breathless Lottie, bursting with news that demanded our immediate attention. This entrance did not impress me, in the middle as I was of a particularly tricky sketch of an angel. I began to frown as she emptied her purchases of black jacks and sherbert flying saucers on to my masterpiece.

On seeing the commotion Alice stood, hand on hip, waiting to see what Lottie had brought back. From the blackened evidence staining her lips and tongue, I suspected she'd eaten most of what she'd bought on the way home. We knew she had something exciting to tell us, but we all remained stubbornly silent, listening to her chew her way through the remaining black jacks.

Alice sat down, delicately tucking her legs beneath her and resting her chin on her hands waiting for Lottie to begin. Alice always did this; she was angry with her sister one moment, and the next indulged her by listening to her ridiculous tales and laughing in all the right places. I'm surprised that I didn't notice then when it was so obvious, the great difference between the two sisters which is now so pronounced in my memory. Lottie with her red hair plastered across her face, and Alice with her black curls neatly piled around her pale face which was as calm as Lottie's was excited. I might have seen Uncle Ted's gentle manner in Alice's graceful ways, and his charm in the flick of her smile. But then, I wasn't looking for it.

Lottie paused now that she had an audience and sighed, waiting for me to look up, then opened her wide smile which was purply-black from the sweets and announced with gravity, "I've had an adventure."

We said nothing, waiting despite ourselves for her to continue.

"I met the yobbos."

This revelation met with a heavy silence. The 'yobbos', though never seen, were known to hang out on the corner of the street. Our imagined picture of them, built up over many years, had developed into one of such horror that it was usually reason enough for us to go the penny shop only in a group. Alice had let Lottie go alone; I scanned her face for signs of guilt, but she was watching her sister, her patient smile a puzzle to me and the encouragement her sister needed.

"What they look like?" gasped Sam.

Ignoring him, she continued. "They beat people up, I seen them."

"Saw them," corrected Alice.

I didn't know whether to be horrified or impressed. Uncle Joe rattled the pages of his *Irish Times*, and we were reminded momentarily that he was there. Lottie glanced over at him before continuing.

"The yobbos," she said, pausing dramatically, "were at the shrine and I think they murdered someone."

"Did you see them do it?" asked Alice eventually. Lottie merely smiled at her sister with her head cocked to one side.

"Was there blood?" asked Sam excitedly.

Barely giving him a glance she said, "Lots. And what's more, look what I found." She put her hand into her pocket and pulled out a set of teeth. "They punched his gob out!"

We gasped staring at the yellowing teeth in her hand. Sam could hardly contain his astonishment, and Lottie placed them in the middle of the table with a triumphant flourish.

Alice said, "How do you know it was the yobbos?"

Dismayed for a second that her story was being doubted, Lottie lowered her voice and became serious. "The saint told me," she said.

This was a new and rather intriguing angle.

"Saint?" asked Alice.

"The one on the landing," she replied without hesitation.

It took some moments before we realised that Uncle Joe had lowered his paper and was looking at us. Then he got up and rushed out of the room. As we all watched him, our mouths open, Lottie dragged Alice up by her arm.

"Come on, I'll show you," she said, and we all trooped out.

On the second landing there was a saint whose name I didn't know. She held a pair of pincers in one hand and a feather in the other; a flowing green robe fell from her plaster brown hair to her tiny sandalled feet.

"Who is it?" Sam shrieked behind us, still clutching his crayons.

"St Appollonia," said a voice behind us. "Patron saint

of dentists, and," Nana continued, "of false teeth."

Lottie's protests as she was bundled down the stairs to make her explanations could be heard all the way from where we sat. Sam said, "Lottie's very brave isn't she?"

As soon as Uncle Joe was given his teeth back, we were all banned to our room where Lottie filled in the rest of the story. She'd known all along, she said, that they were Uncle Joe's teeth, and she'd rescued them from the yobbos because the saint had told her to.

Years later, when Nana died, Lottie and I went back to Cork for the first time since that summer. As we were clearing out one of her dusty boxes of 'treasure', we found the teeth wrapped in tissue at the bottom of a leather case. Lottie laughed and holding them up to the light said that she had in fact taken them from the glass in the bathroom and carried them around with her all morning until an opportunity presented itself for an adventure. I watched her, still seeing the child proud of her find, but knowing that it belonged to a different time. She suddenly stopped laughing and put the teeth back where we found them. We said nothing to each other as we went downstairs.

Uncle Ted eventually arrived at two o'clock, his pockets full of sweets. He picked each one of us up and swung us round; only Alice stood demurely by, preferring the dignity of a hug to the wild "Me! Again! Again!" yelled by Sam as he ran round behind us never realising when the game had stopped. The sun had been gloomy all morning, but as we drove to Kinsale, it came through orange and sunny with only the faintest glowering of a storm.

We spent an hour running around the grounds of the fort, watching the hippies who lived beneath its arches, wondering as we peered into their squatters' rooms, what it must be like to be eighteen. Alice sat on the grass next to Uncle Ted picking at daisies and singing to herself whilst Lottie and I ran along the grassy banks of the fort with Sam as our dragon, teasing him mercilessly until he began to cry. Uncle Ted sat listening to the World Service on a small radio which he carried with him everywhere. He rolled and smoked his strong cigarettes, whistling along with Alice, and occasionally getting up to see if we were still there whilst amusing Sam with stories when he wandered over to complain about Lottie and me.

After a while, we sat on blankets and drank bottles of Tanora, warm and only slightly fizzy after hours of being stored in a hot car. Uncle Ted told us about the ghost of the White Lady which haunted the walls of the fort, a victim of unrequited love who'd thrown herself to death hundreds of years before. Lottie, unimpressed by a story of which she was not the author, began to question him: when had she died and who had found her? What was her real name and what did she look like? Alice nudged her, "Ssh, we want to hear," but Lottie was already in full flow now, talking about the saint, a story which I knew would become more absurd each time it was told. Uncle Ted laughed so much that I thought he must have known about Uncle Joe's teeth but no one else was listening.

It was Alice who wanted to go down to the quay. Nana had told her about seeing the fishermen bringing in an octopus when she was a girl. Alice had never seen an octopus, so Uncle Ted indulged her as he always did, and we found ourselves trooping off in a reluctant line towards the sea.

The harbour was quiet, with a few boats bobbing up and down under the darkening sky. Sam was blubbering about being cold which kept Uncle Ted busy pointing things out to distract him, "There's a fishing boat," he said, and, "That's a lighthouse." Lottie, who was beginning to get very bored, kept turning to me and rolling her eyes claiming she could see whales in the water. Alice edged her way carefully along the quay wall, peering into the water some several feet below, stopping every few feet to squint over the stone as a ripple or a splash caught her attention. I think I remember feeling the first drop of rain touch my cheek.

The storm seemed to come from nowhere, the sea, hitting the wall in short bursts, kept time with the rain, rocking the boats like toys. There was hardly anyone about. We had wandered down to the far edge of the quay where it jettied out into the sea. Uncle Ted tried to roll a cigarette in the shelter of the sea wall whilst trying to grab Sam who was running up and down with Lottie. I saw Alice at the end of the jetty. Turning to us, she grinned and pointed at the lightning which forked into the sea some miles off shore. Uncle Ted shouted to her to keep back. Lottie and Sam were fighting, yelling at each other, and I turned to help Uncle Ted keep them under control. Sam suddenly shot out from under my grasp, his sweater slipping through my fingers. I ran after him, Lottie taunting, which brought a sharp slap from Uncle Ted that silenced her for a few moments. In the midst of all this commotion, we had forgotten about Alice. If there was a noise somewhere behind us, nobody heard it.

The gulls were everywhere and in the growing deluge their screams drowned out her name. Uncle Ted ran frantically up and down the quay, looking over the edge, stopping, wheeling round, screaming his daughter's name. We huddled beneath the shelter of the harbour master's house watching him, suddenly subdued, knowing neither what to do nor where to go.

He turned and came racing towards us. Gathering Sam in his arms, he rushed us to the first building on the harbour road, the White Lady Cafe. His eyes stared wild and cold through the rain, he had no jacket and his hair stuck to his face as he ran. Sam's mouth was open in silent protest and Lottie and I held tightly to each other's hands, terrified in case we should lose sight of him forever. In the cafe we were told to sit down and to wait. I heard Uncle Ted tell a lady with yellow hair at the till to ring the police and something else, then he ran back outside and down to the quay. I craned my neck to watch until I lost him in the mist and fog of the window. The lady came over and gave us each a glass of milk and a cake with a cherry on the top.

"You children'll be freezing," she said and ruffled Sam's hair.

"Of course she's prob'ly got kidnapped," Lottie began after a minute or two. The woman was watching her.

"There'll be a ransom," she whispered under her breath to me.

"No there won't!" I snapped.

"What's a ransom?" said Sam.

"Millions and millions..." she went on, but even she lost heart and slumped back in her chair turning the base of her glass round and round.

"Where's Uncle Ted gone?" wailed Sam, and the woman came over with more cakes to divert us.

Lottie said, "Maybe she fell in," then sat forward in her chair and folded her arms, resting her chin on them the way Alice would.

"Tell us a story Lottie," I urged her.

"Yes!" said Sam, his eyes lighting up.

"I don't know any stories," she said.

I saw cars with flashing lights race past the window, there were a lot of people milling around beyond the glass where before there had been none. Sam asked lots of questions and the lady told us they were looking for our sister.

"She's my sister," said Lottie. Outside, the road sparkled with the warmth of the rain, the evening bringing the end of the storm.

It was dark when Uncle Ted came back. The storm was over.

He sat down heavily and the woman asked him if he wanted a cup of tea. He just nodded staring at the table. I remember Uncle Ted as a tall, handsome man with sparkling eyes which lit up his whole face when he laughed. He had a gentle manner that produced a certain awkwardness emphasised by his large hands and ambling gait. That day, all his qualities were swallowed up in the image of his strong shoulders stooped over and his hands feverishly lifting cigarette after cigarette to his silent mouth. He looked up at each of us from under his lashes, almost as though he didn't know who we were. His jeans, baggy around his narrow hips and his rough linen shirt soaked to the skin made him look extraordinary.

The door opened and a policeman in a wet oilskin coat popped his head through the door, caught sight of Uncle Ted, then signalled to him with a nod. Uncle Ted raised his hand in acknowledgement and turned to look at us. We wanted him to tell us one of his wild tales, to make us laugh. Above all, we wanted him to be the man, in the space of a few hours, he no longer was. I had overheard Nana call him, "A typical bloody Irishman." I didn't know what she meant, but in those few minutes, there in the cafe, they were the only words I could hear in my head and somehow they didn't seem to fit the man I saw before me.

"Your ma'll be here soon," he said to Lottie, and followed the policemen out into the brightening air.

When we got home the lights were all blazing in the front room. I could vaguely make out the shapes of Nana and Uncle Joe in the lamplight, but there were several other shapes I didn't recognise. Uncle Ted and Aunty Maeve had stayed in Kinsale, Mum had brought us back to Cork and bought us chips on the way home. We never had chips, Nana said the smell made her feel sick. Something was badly wrong but not even Sam asked what it was.

Sam, Lottie and I were not taken into the front, instead we were ushered upstairs to the bathroom and its big white sink with rough corners and Uncle Joe's teeth in the glass on the shelf. When we went into the bedroom a soft light cast shadows on the floorboards and the pile of toys and clothes strewn carelessly around. I thought I could hear soft breathing, barely audible; I looked into the room but there was no one there.

Sometime in the middle of the night I opened my eyes to see Alice standing at the window looking down into the wet deserted street. I slipped out of bed and tiptoed over to her.

"Who were all those people downstairs?" I asked. She didn't answer.

The room had an amber glow from the streetlamps which I could see below, level with the lower windows. I could see right across the city, the yellow dots of the lamps spread out like a chain of baubles. The front door slammed below and I craned my neck to see as Uncle Ted's car drove slowly away. I wondered if Alice had seen him, but she was no longer there. Not beside me, nor in the big bed where Lottie was snoring with her red hair tangled about her. I stayed where I was, looking out across the sleeping city as I heard footsteps on the landing.

extract from

the handbook of the ark
(living through the next millenium and beyond)

francis mead

francis mead has taught
english to palestinians on
the west bank, pioneered a
new approach to toilet-
training, studied at the
sorbonne, produced and
presented arts programmes
on bbc world service, spent
a year in psychotherapy,
and owned a fiat 126. he is
6 foot tall, peroxide blonde,
and will provide a photo if
required. seeks attractive,
slim, non-scene publisher.
(non-smoker preferred but
not essential.)

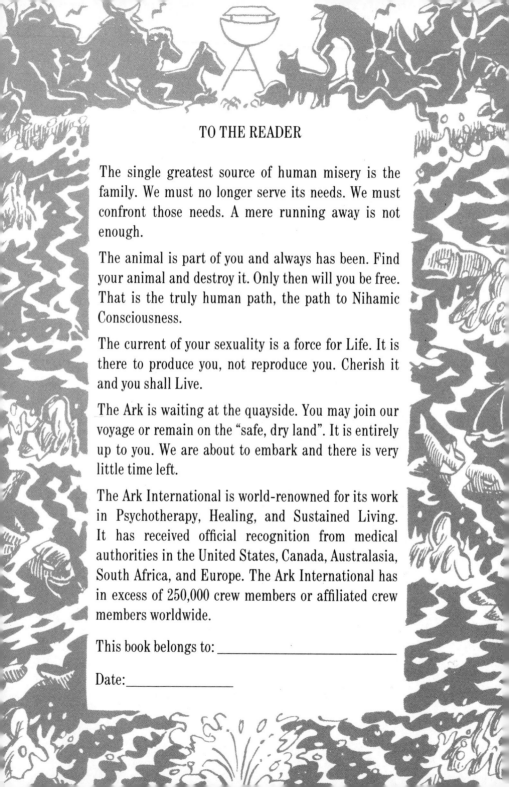

TO THE READER

The single greatest source of human misery is the family. We must no longer serve its needs. We must confront those needs. A mere running away is not enough.

The animal is part of you and always has been. Find your animal and destroy it. Only then will you be free. That is the truly human path, the path to Nihamic Consciousness.

The current of your sexuality is a force for Life. It is there to produce you, not reproduce you. Cherish it and you shall Live.

The Ark is waiting at the quayside. You may join our voyage or remain on the "safe, dry land". It is entirely up to you. We are about to embark and there is very little time left.

The Ark International is world-renowned for its work in Psychotherapy, Healing, and Sustained Living. It has received official recognition from medical authorities in the United States, Canada, Australasia, South Africa, and Europe. The Ark International has in excess of 250,000 crew members or affiliated crew members worldwide.

This book belongs to: _____

Date:_____

francis mead

Dictated. 21 October, 2021.

I'M GOING to die. You're going to die. We're going to die. They're going to die. He's going to die/she's going to die.

I'm going to die.

It's taken a considerable amount of time and effort to formulate that little, insistent phrase. My mouth has to work hard. First it opens wide, then my lips close perfectly on each other in two moist hemicircles, they pout for an instant, there's a little spit for the "t", and finally pull back again for the open glide of the "die": "I'm going to die."

But then again, "I'm not going to die," is only slightly more difficult.

Where am I? I'm lying in bed. I have my eyes closed. But there are several things I'm certain of. For instance, I know there's an iron bed-frame just above my head. It has yellow paint on it, which has flaked. The lighting is still a little too bright, even with my eyes closed. And I've pulled the bedclothes to one side because it's very warm in here. I'm not hungry.

The main point of the exercise though is to tell you what happened to the Ark, and to me. I'll come to that in a second. I have help on hand, namely a capable secretary and also a detailed, rather dog-eared manuscript which is in my bedside cabinet. I touched it a few minutes ago. It was okay. I'm very glad they've let me keep it.

Now the Ark. By which I mean the organisation called the Ark International, led by the "No-No Noah". Look it up in the encyclopaedias if you haven't heard of him: the "no taxes and no children" guru. We first came to notice because of a campaign by an animal rights group. You'll see the logic of that a little later.

I think it's best to begin at Birmingham airport. Let me just focus for a minute.

I think the primary feeling was anxiety, extreme anxiety. Things were in a very bad way and I needed to act quickly. I was waiting at a place called the "Travellers Return Bar", a very unpleasant affair – tiny ledge for your coffee, nowhere to sit down. I remember I was just about to take a sip from my espresso when I heard Adam C call to me. There was a kind of high chirp and I turned round, and there he was, striding towards me.

I was frankly embarrassed: even at that stage I hadn't really got used to seeing Ark officers in a public setting. I was wearing an ordinary suit, but he was in the full-length yellow robe, complete with hood. The animal designs were in resplendent orange: parrots, whales, camels, cheetahs, deer. It was far too colourful for him. His face was long and grey and the yellow folds flapped against him as he walked. He was as thin as a pipe-cleaner and his very large feet dragged up little eddies of black dust with each step.

We formally touched shoulders and he produced a

heavy, brown envelope from the pouch at the front of his robe. I was surprised by this but I thought it was better to wait until I was in the car, so I followed him outside. One of the old Jaguars was at the kerb. I remember fumbling with the seal as we pulled away. Inside was the manuscript.

The first thing that caught my eye was the familiar greeting from Cham B.

The Ark International Centre
Trefriw near Machynlleth
· Powys
Wales 2BC 3NO

Tel: 0654 32
Fax: 0654 34

The Great Depth Beneath   10 a.m. September 6, 1999

Welcome Simon A, Keeper of the Ark!
Only myself, Mason S, Aaron L, Helen O, and Elder Sem V know of the contents of this document. Adam C has simply been told that you have an important appointment with The Builder tonight to discuss European sales. I will explain.

Not long after I spoke to you this morning Helen O discovered that one of the review discs had been tampered with. Sections of the new Handbook had been removed and replaced with extracts from The Builder's private journal or at least what *appears* to be his private journal. Other messages had also been inserted in the body of the text.

A further search revealed that a second disc had been tampered with. Our problem is that a few discs had already been sent to newspapers, medical bodies, and broadcasters. So a corrupt version of the Handbook could have got out.

The intention is obvious: someone, a crew member or an outsider, intends to sabotage the Ark by discrediting us. Given the current speculation in the press, a leakage of spurious "information" about The Builder could be extremely damaging. We have to find out who is responsible.

Events are moving quickly. As I write, search parties are out in pursuit of the overboards. Their cabins are being thoroughly examined.

So this is your task. Use your journey to examine the printout closely. (We have marked the insertions.) Attempt to establish if there is any pattern in the suppressions and deletions. Build up a profile of the likely ringleaders and bring me an assessment of how their treacherous plot was carried out. Be ready to assist with interrogation if the overboards are located.

We trust you will not fail us.

We will proceed with further annotations of the text and bring you news as we receive it.

The Tide is Rising! In the name of Adra-Hasis The Builder
Cham B, Third Son of the Ark.

francis mead

Dictated. 21 October, 2021.

I'd been very lucky. Quite unwittingly, Cham had provided me with a "Handbook" that seemed specially designed to further my plans. My only problem was car sickness induced by a combination of cigarette smoke and the smell of polished leather. But I quickly settled into a routine: I was like a diver, plunging into the text for a few minutes and then surfacing again to take breath and look out of the window.

I peered through the heavy rain and discovered we were already off the motorway for some reason. I turned the page. It was as if The Builder was sending me a message: the Ark could still be saved.

THE HANDBOOK OF THE ARK

INTRODUCTION

Call me Niham. Call me Ut-Napishtim, Xisuthros, Adra-Hasis, Noah, Noe. I am all those names: I am The Builder of the Ark. And so could you be. "Niham" means "to give rest" in Ancient Hebrew and I am here to comfort you. But I can only bring comfort if you show me your pain.

What is Life? One thing's for certain: it's not "life". Life is not "life". Let's take a look at "life" first, and let me ask an easy question. What would you have if you took a scorecard and filled out the most significant events of an average "life" once it was all over? I'll give you two examples. We'll call them Robin and Diana.

ROBIN'S SCORECARD:

1 Born. 2 Weaned at nine months (mild protest). 3 Parents divorce at fifteen. 4 Becomes estate agents' clerk at eighteen. 5 Marries Diana at twenty, two children. 6 Sees parents every Christmas and Sunday. 7 Parents die (surprised at how little he's affected). 8 Retires at sixty-five, takes up sketching church furniture. 9 Completes study of The Victorian Pew. 10 Bored by long country walks with wife. 11 Operation for enlarged prostate at sixty-nine. 12 Dies of prostate cancer in a fog of pain-killing drugs aged seventy-one (his daughter the only one to weep at funeral, son surprised at how little he is affected).

DIANA'S SCORECARD:

1 Born. 2 Regarded as responsible girl, "good with her two younger brothers." 3 Parents say she will be a wonderful mother. 4 Attends secretarial college at sixteen. 5 Becomes company secretary at local estate agents, aged nineteen. 6 Marries Robin ("warm, gentle man"), two children. 7 Joins amateur dramatic society at forty-eight. 8 Discovers that two friends at society are most important people in her life. 9 Bored by long country walks with husband. 10 Delighted at husband's death (shocked by her reaction). 11 Breaks hip at seventy (furious that she's slowing down). 12 Dies of coronary thrombosis at seventy-five (in ambulance she feels it is far too early and wonders how she wasted so much of her life with an ineffectual man).

NUMBERS

So that is "life". It's all done by numbers: 17, 82, 34, 48. Just a question of mathematics and a final figure – probably between 70 and 80. And that's it: in the end, despite all our secret rage and terror, we meekly give in to the tyranny of those numbers. The numbers crunch us.

But there is another Way – a Way I want to show you. The key is not in healthy diets, exercise or vitamin pills, although all those things can contribute. No. The key is to choose Life. You must help us. For God's sake help us. You don't know what is going on here. The onboards are the victims. We have not hurt anybody. They want us to disappear. Sounds absurdly simple doesn't it? Yes, it *is* absurdly simple: but that doesn't mean it isn't extremely difficult to do.

Imagine, if you can, a world without those numbers. Just try something for me: take your watch off. Or, if you haven't got a watch, cover over any clock that you can see. Think of the peace that your body and mind are aching for. You are free of time. You don't have to rush any more for that appointment. There's no need to hurry out to the shops before they close. There's just peace. Imagine not looking at your watch for several hours, for several days, for several months. Imagine living a life without that watch, ticking away faintly, always just audible. You can Live like that. Be calm, be peaceful. Be free. That's how we all Live on the Ark. You can join us.

Dictated. 21 October, 2021.

I looked up again. We were queuing to get back on the motorway. The rain was continuous.

I was surprised by the panicky tone in the women's message. Had they really thought The Builder wanted them to *disappear*? I found that inconceivable, but I hadn't seen his private journal and they had. I began to wonder about the leader of the Ark. I read on.

THE UNHOLY TRINITY

Let me take you on a journey to the most dangerous, terrifying, and mysterious place in the world: THE FAMILY. Where, after all, are we most likely to encounter murder, rape, abuse, grievous bodily harm, cruelty, humiliation, the unaccountable abuse of power, slavery, emotional blackmail, dishonesty, betrayal, wounding contempt, hatred, boredom, frustration, fatigue, deadening of the spirit, and sheer waste of energy? But, encouraged by Freud, we have been obsessed with the family this century. Mothers and fathers and sisters and brothers and sons and daughters and mothers and fathers again. And again. Always our mothers and fathers.

So what to do? We could just say, "To Hell with it! Let's dump the family and move on and be free of it all." Alas! Experience teaches us it isn't that easy. This is the problem: the more we try to cut our family ties by simply running away, the more we are bound by them. To our horror the family creeps up on us when we are least expecting it. We suddenly find ourselves repeating the same old lines from a play that has already been written for us. And so we go on. Until we die.

The truth is that we have to go back to go forward. We have to face the family, know it in its full horror. Freud wasn't mistaken in saying that the family is the source of our current ills, but he was wrong when he told us to return to it. That is exactly what we must not do.

To be truly free of the family is to live in a revolutionary state, far more revolutionary than anything the Bolsheviks ever dreamed up. Each of us could be free, autonomous and accountable only to ourselves. We may choose to establish friendly contact with foreign powers, but there would never be invasion of our territory or colonial control. This state we call Nihamic Consciousness.

SPILLING THE SEED

Now it is time to uncover the second great evil that plagues us. What is the cornerstone of this failed and corrupt institution that we know as the family? Why are we supposed to band together with a mate and devote all our lives to its autocratic demands? The answer, I'm sure, is obvious: PROCREATION.

Procreation is almost universally described as the creation of life. But that is false. The opposite is true: procreation ensures our death. Not only in global terms where it is clear that continuing, widespread procreation is a mortal danger to us all, but each individual is uniquely threatened by the demand, the requirement, to procreate. *Thou shalt procreate. Thou shalt go forth and multiply.* And verily we have done. And how! But it is, I repeat, the death of us. Why is that?

If he could *only* have practised what he preached! None of us would have been unhappy. None of this would have happened.

Aging is a little understood phenomenon. Biologists notoriously fail to agree over its causes and consensus seems as far away as ever. Most of their energy is devoted to a search for the mythical gene, the illusory biological "fault" that causes us to sicken and die. They are on a wild-goose chase. All the time, the key to mortality is right under their noses: it is the pernicious association of sexual intercourse with procreation. Death is *not* determined by some spurious genetic mechanism: our lives are in our own hands.

In each sexual act that is aimed at conception there is an unconscious overspill, something left on the side, a giving away of an essential part of ourselves. It is not only the exhausting process of bringing up children that depletes us, it is the very act of engendering them.

Our vital energy, channelled through sexual desire, has to be kept within a closed system. If we are to Live on, we must make sure of one thing: we must keep this vital sexual energy within the closed system that is the Self. If it is channelled correctly it becomes a never-ending, renewable energy resource, the key to a healthy existence. But once fertilisation is our aim, the closed system is broken and we are subtly expended.

★ ★ ★

NIHAMIC CONSCIOUSNESS IS ALL ABOUT CHOICES. WE CAN CHOOSE TO BE LIBERATED FROM THE THINGS THAT KILL US.

★ ★ ★

To confirm the conviction, built up over many years of experience and observation, that there has been a massive drain on our life-giving sexual energy, we commissioned a highly respected team of physicists to carry out a controlled study on a selected group of volunteers. The aim was to assess the potential energy, expressed in joules, that each individual can take advantage of, *provided the sexual act is not directed towards procreation.*

To give you a meaningful idea of the figure they came up with try to imagine, if you can, the actual quantity of sexual activity that, by the law of averages, must be taking place in the world at this very moment. By our calculations, there are 3 million people making love to each other even as you read these words. Three million active sets of sexual organs.

Now, applying the results of our study, it has been shown that the amount of energy being expressed in these sexual acts would be enough to light and heat a large city say the size of Manchester or Seattle or Melbourne for six months! It is *that* sort of energy that we must learn to harness for ourselves.

THE THIRD EVIL

The third of the Unholy Trinity and the ideal that binds them all together is LOVE. Not love for ourselves, or for mankind in general, but ROMANTIC LOVE. Never have we created such a suspect ideal, one that has led us astray and let us down so often.

Look at the mess that "relationships", never mind marriage, are in. I ask you honestly, how many truly happy relationships can you name among people you know? Have you thought for a moment? How many have you found?

80

Romantic love was, of course, invented in order to serve the twin institutions of marriage and procreation. This was in an age when it was necessary for humans to breed to ensure the survival of the species. We must recognise that we have entered a new and different stage in our history. But old habits die extremely hard!

Again it is a matter of choice. The choice we've plumped for has shaped our values, our experience of everything we do. We have exhausted ourselves trying to build an ideal home: it's called "the monogamous relationship", and we continue to insist that it's built to last until death. But we are puzzled, very puzzled, at our extraordinary inability to stop the roof leaking, burglars breaking in every other week and the bailiffs finally coming to repossess the property.

The answer to this is also bafflingly simple: we don't have to keep up the crippling mortgage payments on this house! We think we won't be happy without the "stability", "the loving bond", "the intimacy" of relationships. But I repeat, this is patently contradicted by the facts. We can choose another way of living, far less stressful, far less draining – a Way that enables us to Live.

It is no secret that not a single full member of the Ark International has ever died. This is the single biggest lie all. Why is that? Because those who achieve full Nihamic Consciousness have freed themselves from the three great evils: FAMILY, PROCREATION, and LOVE.

francis mead

Dictated. 22 October, 2021.

Family, procreation, and love. When I'd finished the manuscript I flipped back to that page for a last glance. The three great evils.

The car was already dipping down towards the lake. I remember resting my head on the seat again. We pulled round on the gravel and the gangplank appeared above me. I could see rows of white droplets swinging beneath each of the iron bars.

Adam came round the side of the car. I didn't want to get out straight away but he pulled the door open before I could move. Afterwards, I felt grateful to him. I think he helped me make my decision. I had to stand up and give him instructions. Maybe it was the clean air as well. Whatever it was, by the time I'd got to my feet, I knew exactly what I wanted to do. I told Adam to park the car and turned to look up at the Ark itself. The damp timbers had turned black.

I first heard the shouting when I reached the upper gangplank. Somewhere deep beneath me was a continuous, heavy thudding.

Family, procreation, and love had been successfully banished. My task was to bring discipline, animal vigour, and sexual energy in their place.

THE NEW MILLENIUM WAS ABOUT TO BEGIN.

addictionary

melanie danburg

melanie a danburg was born in 1969 in houston, texas. she studied creative writing and american studies at the university of california, santa cruz; and has lived in england for two years. her stories, articles, and poems have been printed in various extremely small publications.

WALTER REYNOLDS, historian, had intended to stick with Alexander Hamilton, statesman, throughout. He was determined to show it all: the intrigue, the romance, the blackmail. The passion of the man. The deceit of the woman. The life of post-revolutionary Philadelphia.

(W. Reynolds relating his research's raison d'être:)

"I'm engrossed in the idea that Alexander Hamilton was pulled into the affair with Maria Reynolds. It's obvious that the Secretary of the Treasury was an easy target for blackmail in the Philadelphia of 1791. His social standing and vulnerability were equally high. I'm questioning how much the mudslinging newspaper war between Hamilton and the followers of Jefferson was a cover to distract the public from character sullies. I believe it was. I believe in the purity of Alexander Hamilton and the demoralizing influence of Maria Reynolds, family connections aside."

melanie danburg

The demise of Walter's dedication to his work happened to coincide with the rise of his friendship with Freya Hirsch, bookseller. Their climb had been leisurely at first; a day's outing, a browse and a chat in her academic book store. Enthused by their friendship, he started dropping by daily to discuss the new facts that contributed to his thesis. She kept an eye on the latest history publications, giving him inside information on academic publishing in Philadelphia. Anything 200 years old was invaluable to him. They flirted intellectually. He was smitten. And when, finally, he was at the point of writing, she waited casually to hear about his pen-to-paper work. She expected him to ask her advice about organization, focus, potential publishers. But he was silent. For Walter Reynolds' good intentions had slipped away. It all started with ‹schism›. Then, after that first regression down to ‹schist›, the dictionary gradually eroded his interests, his thoughts, everything about him. Noah Webster, lexicographer, had managed to surpass Freya Hirsch, bookseller, in Walter's estimation.

(Walter's shamefaced sidetracking soliloquy:)

"I was in the final stages of my research, and I was planning the progression of my monograph. Everything was orderly, my thesis proven, my notes supportive, the correct quotes ready for the correct paragraphs. I only needed the final outline to organize my structure before I began the actual writing. For some historians, this is the easiest phase, the most captivating aspect of research. Personally, I prefer the initial rush of enthusiasm for a project, the delight of going through documents in search of vital information. At any rate, I was ready to finish up this particular project and I devised a title for the work. I called it: 'Schism or Diversion?: Alexander Hamilton's public war with Thomas Jefferson, viewed in light of his private liaison with Maria Reynolds.' It was at this stage that I found I simply couldn't spell the word ‹schism›. There are a few words which have affected me thus, notably: cinnamon, imbecile, and gazpacho. I'm sure there are others, but these are three that remained, from youth, unspellable. And now, I was forced to add another, more vital word to the list. I was compelled to look it up every time I needed it. After a few days my pocket dictionary opened to it automatically."

Enough. His words go on and on. His point was that he'd lost that spark of passion about his work, and he was basically ready to wander off with whatever project came along next. So, in came the dictionaries. How did the dictionaries affect his attitude? It started with just the occasional word catching his eye. All of those unfamiliar combinations that guide the dictionary reader through the alphabet. Okka. Sciolistic. Minacious. Cystotomy. Paleography. Flyte. Rhizopus. All the way from A to Zymurgy, in the "Second College Edition" of *Webster's New World Dictionary*. He gradually descended into the dense red book, spending the hours he should have been devoting to his thesis, instead counting words. He came up with absurdities.

(From pages penned '~~Skhi~~ Schism or Diversion —Thesis Notes')

"What were Hamilton's goals in perpetuating the quarrel with Jefferson? How should I qualify my theory that he was trying to quell the rumors about Maria Reynolds with publicized ~~quarolus querolcs~~ querulousness?—There are eighty-eight entries in the pocket dictionary for ‹Q›. The best ones after ‹querulousness› are ‹quinsy› and ‹Quonset hut›. I have a quinsy now. I have never seen a Quonset hut, as far as I know."

And with Walter on the words, he couldn't stop. He couldn't leave them alone. Here Freya Hirsch truly entered into the picture. He turned to her in search of Webster's *Grammatical Institute*. This tome was the first attempt by an American, the notable Noah Webster, to define English as a language for the new nation. It was a ten day wait for the order to arrive, and in the meantime Walter was to dedicate himself to the completion of the Hamilton essay. It had originally been planned as a hundred and fifty page investigation of the interrelationship of the newspaper wars and the Reynolds' blackmail. Already he had reduced it to seventy pages, at most: barely an acknowledgment of the work he'd put into the research. Walter did little to produce his pedantic pamphlet, other than writing a short paragraph crediting the role of Hamilton in his original distraction.

(Walter whitewashing the waning of his work:)

"Much of my new enthusiasm began with Hamilton, himself a man of extensive vocabulary. I've consulted *Webster's* sporadically while reading Hamilton's letters and papers, when I needed to clarify passages like: 'I have often heard that authors in England, or their booksellers for them, when they find their books do not sell according to their wishes, hire some garretteer to write against them—then publish a reply to his own lucubrations—and so go on, objecting and replying, until the attention of the public is drawn towards the book, and thus it is brought into demand.' Actually, ‹lucubrations› isn't in my pocket dictionary. But ‹lubber› is: a clumsy person."

Walter needed to be cut off, to be controlled in his fancies. But the hiatus, while he waited for the book, didn't calm him. He began to feverishly question Freya Hirsch about words, looking through the complete OED she kept in the register showcase. His lengthy visits and frequent compliments piqued her interest. She wanted to know if he needed the Webster in some connection to Hamilton. Both men were, after all, Federalists. Perhaps Webster had contributed to Hamilton's diatribes in the *Gazette of the United States?* No. Then perhaps he had written to Hamilton with advice about how to handle the affair with Maria? No. Surely Webster didn't include subversive diatribes against the Jeffersonians in his own work? Of course not; the *Blue-Backed Speller* (Part I of *A Grammatical Institute of the English Language*) was published in 1783, a full decade before the controversy began. So why the sudden shift in focus? Why Webster?

(An affronted answer to Freya's axiomatic apple of discord:)

"Why should I persist with Alexander Hamilton? When he got involved with Maria Reynolds he was veering from the path that drew me to him in the first place. Admittedly, I was initially fascinated by Hamilton; but the precisely controlled, adamantly ambitious man risked his sterling reputation in his flagrant flirtations. Noah Webster had no such flaws. He did not deliberately misconstrue the words of imagined foes; he worked to create a national unity for Americans. He rejected the aristocratic systems of England and brought education to the thousands of students wondering what the new national identity would mean to their futures."

That last bit of Walter's was a lie; an attempt to justify his own retrogression by praising the virtues of a man he, as yet, knew little about. He simply got carried away with the novelty of language. Tragically, the *Speller* was delayed at the distributors, but he frittered away the time by reading Freya Hirsch's dictionaries and writing her love missives. He wanted her to be amazed at his own way with words. And she was fittingly flattered. In his previous diatribes about the

Hamilton thesis, she had concluded that Walter didn't know what he was talking about. So going up a new path might not be such a big mistake. And maybe his study of the lexicographer would help de-anti-quate his own language.

(Wally's longing love letter to lively, laudable Freya Hirsch:)

"My dear Miss Hirsch,

You must forgive my audacity in dispatching this unrequested letter. My missive's mission is to relate the visions I have of you: a veritable paragon of pul-chritude. But it is not simply your extraordinary beauty which inspires me whilst penning this epistle. Oh, no! Indeed, your fair visage, though paramount in arousing my interest in you, is secondary to the diurnal joy I feel in contemplating your achievements as a trader of books and, in many senses, as a vessel of culture for all Philadelphia. Your shop is spoken of as an avenue for the attainment of lofty preoccupation and, as you will surmise from my position as an academic, this is a matter I deem to be of the utmost importance. I sincerely desire that my palpable devotion to you will not weigh too heavily upon your conscience. I ask for no more than permission to continue my regular encounters with your exquisite character. With all good faith, I remain,

Yours,
Walter Reynolds."

melanie danburg

Walter's profusion of passionate ‹P› words amused Freya Hirsch, but the visits to the book shop gradually became calls on the OED, not the bookseller. While this freed her up to deal with the paying customers, she began to feel used by the errant historian. He blocked access to her cash register without attempting to entertain her with the etymology of expressions like ‹manse›, ‹sacerdotal›, and ‹gawk›. His pedantic chuckles no longer preceded the phrase, "Miss Hirsch, have you encountered this word before?" Her ire led her to withhold Webster's *Grammatical Institute, Part I*, once it had finally arrived. And when she did present Walter with the volume, he neglected to thank her, ignoring the attached bill for the special order and rushing back to his apartment. He didn't surface in time for their date the next evening.

(Walter's shopping list, from *Speller's* Table XXIX :)

Of Herbs, roots, Plants, Fruits, &c.			
Tur nips	purf lain	gil li flow er	ftraw ber ry
po ta toes	cref fes (f)	fen nel	goofe ber ry
car rots	for rel	dill	grapes
peas	on ion (g)	par fnip	cit rons
beans	gar lic	fmal lage	or an ges
beets (b)	fhal lots	byf fop	rai fins (m)
rad ifh es (c)	leeks	faf fron	lem ons
fpin age	thyme	ap ples	tam a rinds
cab bage	fage	pears	wheat
col ly flow er	wa ter mel on (h)	cher ries	rye
ar ti choke	mufk mel on (h)	plums	corn
af par a gus (d)	cu cum ber (i)	al monds	bar ley
let tuce	pum kin (j)	peach es	oats
en dive	fquafh	figs	grafs
cel e ry (e)	gourds	wal nuts	row en
parf ley	fern	cheft nuts	flax *
	tu lip	fil berts	fpike nard
	vi o let	rafp ber ry (k)	mul len
	pink	bil ber ry (l)	dai fy

—also frozen pizza, milk, tofu, soda, and salsa."

While normally, in an investigation, Walter produced copious notes on his fanciful theories, his reaction
to the *Grammar* was simply to dog-ear the pages whose
lessons most appealed to him. He did occasionally do
more than shop for the common fruits that Webster
indexed. He also copied out the tables, from 'words
of three and four letters' to 'words of five syllables, accented on the fourth.' But writing "cir cum lo cu tion
cir cum val la tion cir cum vo lu tion" was not aimed at
impressing those who read and publish historical
works. Was it the fear of going broke that snapped
Walter out of his rhythmic reverie? Or was he driven
back to the bookseller, eager to share his joy in the
tables and lessons? Did Freya Hirsch actually worry
about Walter in his little apartment, dissolving in the
vat of vocabulary? Was there a mercy mission from
the skirted sibyl, on pretense of an unpaid bill or the
availability of a Webster work? Well, whether she
took pity upon Walter or he pulled himself away from
the *Grammar* in search of the history of one of Webster's words, a consultation with beloved Freya did
occur.

(Walter waxing whimsically on Webster / from
Table XV—words of three syllables, accented on the
first:)

"To an i mate the for ci ble ap ti tude of this cor di al
gen tle man is to in ti mate that to ren o vate the rhet o
ric was a per qui site for par ti san el o quence. He ro
ism was haz ard ous in the change a ble peas ant ry, so

se ri ous crit i cism of ob du rate man u script(s) was lau di ble."

Freya Hirsch's reaction to Walter's transformed lingo—from formal phrases to stilted tricrotics—was to demand accountability from him. What was the point of his absorption in Webster? Would he produce anything from it, or merely babble on about irregular pronunciations and accented vowels? Where was the proof of erudition which he had asserted to her, before losing himself in this blue-backed book? And why bother so much with language if there was no context for it? The emphasis upon nonsense had compounded her changing opinion about Walter. The historian was startled. He hadn't been aware that Freya Hirsch cared overmuch about what he was doing these days. Would she approve if he veered back towards the traditional? If he devoted himself to his essay on Noah Webster's influence in colonial America? Maybe, said the bookseller. Maybe so.

(Walter trying to wean himself from Webster's words / from Table XXVII—short vowels inadequately divided:)

"Op po si tion to my e bul li tion has led to an ad mo ni tion to produce a com po si tion on the rhet o ri cian. It is a pro pi tious and aus pi cious fru i tion to my pe ti tion, on con di tion that I show con tri tion for de fi cient co mi tial of ca pri cious vo li tion. And I must please Freya Hirsch."

94

Walter determined that if even Webster's pocket dictionary didn't include Noah Webster in the index-ical "Hall of Fame of Great Americans," he should bring the man to the attention of the world. And it was true that there was a dearth of material about him; even the brief *Encyclopedia Brittanica* entry on Noah suggested that there needed to be a major study of the man and his goals. Did he intend the influence that he achieved? Was he ambitious for himself or for the new country? Was it revolutionary fervor or insightful genius? But these were the same questions Walter used to ask about Alexander Hamilton. Was history this repetitive, or was it just Walter who was redundant?

(Reynolds' return to ritual research rigidity:)

"The directions in which Noah was headed aimed for a particularly American view of language. The *American Spelling Book* strove to create a uniform pronunciation for the populace, as well as to improve the educational system of the States. As he wrote in 1789: 'As an independent nation, our honor requires us to have a system of our own, in language as well as government. Great Britain, whose children we are, and whose language we speak, should no longer be our standard; for the taste of her writers is already corrupted, and her language on the decline.' To this end he promoted spellings like ‹honor›, without the useless ‹u›. He wanted to rid the language of British affectations. Admirable."

But it wasn't long before Walter felt stifled by the stiffness of summary. Although he had Freya Hirsch actively supporting him—and she even went out to dinner with him weekly while he delved into Webster's *Dissertations*—he already missed his words.

(Walter's self-justifying surge of sensible speech:)

"I am more interested in Noah Webster's way with words than his political goals. His wasn't a public life; he didn't present reports to Congress or write letters to George Washington. His was a quest to organize language, to establish new meanings based upon the country's identity, to promote 'the necessity, advantages and practicability of reforming the MODE of SPELLING, and of rendering the orthography of words correspondent to the pronunciation.' It did have a lot to do with politics, but this fact simply makes it easier for me to undertake a study of the man and his life away from the political limelight. Noah Webster was a great patriot not because of his statesmanship, but because of his educational drive."

Walter, pedantic side again to the fore, reflected upon his propinquity to the lexicographer. Should he move from Philadelphia to New Haven? Attain enlightenment from Webster's resting ground? Freya Hirsch bristled. He had removed himself from his sea of speech shibboleths on her account, suddenly reverted to them, and almost immediately spoke of moving. She denied that she would suffer inordinately from his departure, but she had made an effort because he so patently needed someone to do so. She expected some gratitude. But Walter was carting about an Amtrak timetable as if he might disappear at any moment. And this he did.

(Freya's finespun falderalian farewell from Walter / a selection of Table XII:)

"Doom whom bloom noon prove noose. Choose lose. Who coo two touch botch. Book look. Good should could would soon shoot proud wound. Sprout doubt word, burst thirst flood her worth. Flirt dove, love drop. Swap track tough. Fail fair where they feint brain. Train state straight. Great spake shape, more prose. Known folks rove, none home. Roam globe sworn. Course source know right fight. Smile. While pride guide deep, keep peer read, lead dream. Dear pure, your view true. Use praise phrase. Fond strong once done. Pledge friend. Walter."

extract from

a taxidermist

c j norton

cj norton was born in 1965, a pisces. he went to school in marlow, buckingham- shire. he then proceeded to the university of warwick where he studied film and literature. there he also studied creative writing with playwright, andrew davies. upon leaving university, he worked briefly as a television production assistant then moved on to become an advertising copywriter. this he did for five years, working some of the time in australia. on returning to england he divided his time between freelance copywriting and writing short stories.
he hopes to complete his first novel, *a taxidermist* ex- tracts of which are shown here by the end of 1993.

(i) rhinoceros, 2003

I have a postcard pinned to the wall above my dissecting table. It
has been fixed to this same spot for more than thirty years. Its
edges are ragged and it is smudged with greasy fingerprints from
times when I have felt the need to touch it for inspiration.

The photograph is of a rhinoceros. A female African Black
[*DICEROS BICORNIS*]. She stares from the paper with black glass
eyes. Her two horns are splintered.

When I was a child she frightened me. But she has been so long
in my possession that I look at her and only feel affection now.

(ii) *rhinoceros, 1973*
Pappa told me he was going to see a four hundred year old rhinoceros today. He said she lived in Italy, in a museum. Then he stopped himself and said no, that was not strictly correct. She did not 'live' there at all. She merely gave the appearance of being alive, because she was Stuffed.

I sat on Pappa and Mamma's bed, picking at a hole in Jacko, my toy monkey, swinging my legs, and watching. Pappa was excited about his trip. I could tell from the way he kept on doing and undoing the knot of his tie, his long yellow fingers catching in the material. He had on a brown suit, the one he wore at Aunty Penny's wedding. He looked funny. I was used to seeing him in a brown woolly cardigan and raggedy trousers with stains on them made by the insides of all the animals he worked on.

Mamma came into the room and tutted when she saw him. "You're not going to wear that tatty old thing," she said. "The trousers are too tight."

"I only need to look presentable," Pappa said, trying to pat his bushy hair down. "I'm going to see Aldrovandi's celebrated rhinoceros. I'm not going on a fashion parade."

Pappa would always go on about things like this as if we knew them. Mamma said he was 'wrapped up in his work'. Mamma looked at him, sucking in her cheeks and raising an eyebrow. Turning to me, she said, "Your father is flying away to see another woman. And he's looking like a sack of potatoes."

I said nothing. Mamma was 'acting up' because Pappa had never taken her abroad. All her friends had been away to Spain or France on holiday and come home 'brown as berries'.

"The trouble with your father," Mamma said, talking as if Pappa wasn't in the room, "is that he likes his animals more than his family." Pappa pretended he hadn't heard. He looked at his watch, then at his shiny bag which had B-O-A-C written over it in big blue letters. He moved to the window and pulled back the net curtain. Donald Brim was taking him to the airport and he was frightened of being late.

Turning, Pappa smiled at her. Mamma was still trying to be cross but it wasn't working. "You and your Rhinoceros, Malcolm," she said, walking over to him, putting her hand inside his jacket. They kissed.

When they stopped, Pappa turned to me, picked me up and groaned. "You're getting heavy," he said, pulling me closer until my face was snug against his grey hairy ear. He smelled of soap and toothpaste. "Just how old are you?"

"Five and a half," I answered. I knew Pappa was forty seven and that Mamma was younger, though all she would ever say is Twenty-One Again when I asked. Pappa put me down and stroked my forehead with his finger. "Pappa won't be away long, little man," he said.

Mamma sat on the bed and rubbed her knobbly

knees under her tights. "Derek, why don't you go
Downstairs," she said, "we'll be opening up shop
soon. You can play with the till, you like that."

Pappa looked at his watch again and shook his
head, "Donald will be here soon, Susan."

Mamma got up and stomped to the dressing table.
She sat down and started brushing her hair so quickly
I thought it must be hurting her. I'd brushed her hair
before and it was always tangly.

Pappa sighed and picked up his bag. "Take my hand
Derek," he said. We left Mamma with the brush in her
hands.

As we went down the stairs one by one, Jacko and I
counted each step out loud. Pappa put his hand to his
mouth, coughed and said, "You must look after your
Mamma, Derek. She isn't feeling very well these
days." He whispered, "She's having a Baby. You'll
have a new brother or sister to play with. Would you
like that?"

I nodded, though I wasn't sure. "Will he or she live
in my room?" I asked.

"First in Mamma and Pappa's bedroom, then with
you," Pappa said gently. I wondered where I would
put Jacko and all my toys.

Mamma looked pretty when she came Downstairs
into the shop. Pappa had his face up against the window and his breath was making it foggy. He kept on
talking to himself about traffic, and journey times

from Crouch End to Heathrow.

I was sat on the shop counter, fiddling with the till, making pound and pence signs come up in the glass window.

Mamma took Pappa by the arm and led him over to the shop door. Leaning against the wall, she held him. "I don't want to argue, Malcolm," she said, brushing some white specks from his shoulder. "It's just that Derek needs school clothes, and there's Baby to think of—and this trip is so expensive."

Pappa kissed Mamma on the nose. "You know this is important, Susan," Pappa said in a voice he sometimes used with me. "Aldrovandi was a genius."

"I know," Mamma said and put her head against his shoulder, squeezing him so his jacket wrinkled up.

A car pulled up outside. Mr. Brim honked the horn and waved. I waved back, Mamma didn't. Pappa picked up the case. "Three weeks isn't long," Pappa said as he came over and kissed me. "Remember what I said about helping your Mamma."

I nodded. Pappa then went to kiss Mamma again. He whispered in her ear and chuckled. Mamma laughed. "Be good," he said.

As the door slammed, Pappa started to whistle.

(iii) ᵐ/ₐonkey, 1973
For a place so full of life, Upstairs suddenly seemed empty with Pappa gone. Mamma said it was best we kept busy so she gave Jacko and me chores to do.

We liked dusting the animals best. We would take a yellow rag and some window spray from under the kitchen sink then clomp Downstairs, the blue liquid swishing in its bottle as we went. We would take out a small comb from a drawer under the shop counter, which we used to check for nits.

When Mamma wasn't looking I would spit on the rag and clean the beads in the animals eyes until they sparkled. The shop was so different from Upstairs; it smelled of Pappa and there were so many animals jumbled all together. It was like a Zoo or Safari Park, except all the animals were friends and didn't have to live in cages.

Along the walls there were all sorts of birds-sparrows, ducks, and big birds with pointy beaks with names like Gyr Falcon and Bittern. Some had speckled eggs in with them, others little fish in their mouths. They lived in square cases with grass around their feet. I would spray the glass and polish away, trying to whistle like Pappa.

On the far wall Pappa had hung the big heads of animals which came from Africa. They had funny names like Ibis, Zebra and Gnu. I would comb between their ears and down their long noses, then I would check for bogeys up their snouts. They never had any, though. Next to them was the head of a donkey. It had big droopy ears and was white, with special pink eyes. Pappa called it Al Bino, which I thought was a strange name for a donkey. Al Bino smelled a bit and had fleas until Pappa sprayed him with something called BORAX.

There was one display which Jacko and I didn't like going near. It was a jar with a round top, tucked away in a corner and covered in dust. In it was a little monkey, just like Jacko. He was sat in something that looked like water with bits floating around in it. He was smaller than Jacko and was scrunched up with his legs crossed. His eyes were closed and he had his hands together. Like Christopher Robin saying his prayers. Jacko didn't like him at all, he said. He didn't want to be like that, in the cold water with his eyes closed. It made me feel sad for Jacko and for the monkey in the jar. Whenever we went near it I could see Jacko was frightened—even though his big rubber face was still smiling. I had to hang on to him tightly and go and dust something else.

After the first time we'd dusted all the animals in the shop, I thought we could help by dusting the basement where Pappa did all his Skinning and Mounting, but the door was locked.

Mamma said I was a big help. But even though she said we should all keep busy, she kept on complaining that she felt tired. She would sit at the till, looking through catalogues and putting circles round things, like lampshades and Hi-Fis, with a pencil. Sometimes Mamma would get out a bag of wool and her needles and start knitting. She was making a jumper. One pink one, and one blue one. I didn't like either colour very much and the jumpers looked too small for me. Jacko and I watched her clicking the needles together and tried counting along with her, Knitting One and Purling Two. We didn't know what it meant.

Days passed. The shop was never very busy. Mamma would roll her eyes whenever customers stepped inside the shop and told them to come back when Pappa returned.

Sometimes people came in with their pets, floppy and dead in bags. Mamma booked them in for appointments, telling them to pour alcohol over their animals, wrap them in tin foil, and put them in a cool place 'for the time being'. They were usually upset so Mamma would speak to them in the way she talked to me when I hurt myself. There was a box of tissues by the till in case anyone was crying. Mamma would give some to them so they could dab their noses. She called it her Professional Manner.

One night Mamma made Tea and I sat with Jacko on the sofa and watched the television. A programme was on about Power Strikes. It said there were some men working down the Coal Mines who weren't happy. There were pictures of people in hats with very dirty faces. They looked angry. I thought it must be because they hadn't washed. Then there was a picture of some more men in a desert wearing towels around their heads. I yawned.

Mamma came in with Beefburgers and Chips. As we were eating she said, "Do you miss Pappa?"

I said yes, even though I had a mouthful of Beefburger.

"So do I," she said and was quiet.

In the morning a postcard arrived on the doormat. It was from Pappa. On the front there was a picture of a big black animal with an enormous spiky horn. I read the card. On it were the words:

She is a beauty!

Missing you.

Love Malcolm (Pappa) xxxx

I took the card up to Mamma in bed. She was wearing a blue nightie and didn't look very well. I handed her the card.

As she read it, she started crying. She scrunched up the blanket with her white fingers. I didn't know what to do. I looked down and asked quietly why she was so sad.

"Mamma loves Pappa and Pappa loves a rhinoceros," she said. I climbed onto the bed, put my arms around her neck and hugged her the same way she did when I was upset.

She was still crying when I came back from the bathroom with some toilet paper to mop her tears.

(iv) squirrel, 1979

"Sometimes," Papa said, "people love their pets so much that they want them to live forever. There's nothing wrong in that." We walked down into the basement, Pappa's hand on my back, butterflies in my stomach. "I make their pets perfect again for them," he said.

He lit some tall yellow candles by his workbench. Mamma had phoned earlier. Pappa was angry. "Where are you? Why are you being so irrational?" he shouted down the phone. Pappa couldn't stand people 'being irrational'. I thought his being so upset would put off my introduction to the instruments and their uses. But no such luck.

"I want this to be special for you," Pappa said in his gentlest voice. "People never forget special things." He wasn't angry any more and knew I was nervous.

In a mesh cage placed by the dissecting table a squirrel jumped around on the straw. "I trapped him on The Heath, this morning," Pappa said. Its pink nose twitched furiously, its eyes bright as polished beads. I wanted to stroke him and poked my finger through the mesh.

"Remember, Squirrel will nip if he's cornered," Pappa warned. He began soaping his arms and scrubbing his fingernails. He handed me a bar of wet carbolic soap and told me to do the same. It smelled like the dentists.

"Climb up onto the draining board next to the

workbench." I lifted my nose and sniffed. Brown bottles of ether, camphor, naphthalene, and alcohol with black screw top lids stood before us. Everything was familiar to me, of course, but Pappa had never let me watch him at work. It spoiled his concentration, he said. When he was operating Mamma used to make me stay upstairs in the shop. She'd said I wasn't ready. But now Mamma had gone, Pappa thought it was Time I Learned.

The dissecting table was made of heavy timber and stood on trestles. While Pappa arranged his tools, I ran my finger over the scored surface where he performed his surgery: rasp marks, pin-holes, ingrained dental plaster, alum powder, and dried blood made their own map on the wood. I committed every mark on the table to memory. Soon I would be adding my own marks, I thought. I felt a little queasy.

With a crack of his knuckles, Pappa pulled on a pair of thin white rubber gloves. Some white powder fell from them as he wriggled his wrist inside. I noticed from the jar that it was Mamma's talcum powder. She must have left it behind.

Pappa removed a glass stopper from a bottle and doused a wad of cotton wool with the solution. "Ether," Pappa said. A smell, like Victory Vs, broke across the air. Pappa unpinned the cage door and removed Squirrel by the scruff of his neck.

"The subject will still have fleas in his coat. We'll deal with them later." All of a sudden Pappa was talking to me like he talked to his taxidermist friends.

Squirrel squirmed and flailed his legs, but Pappa held firm. With a pair of tweezers he picked up the ether-soaked wad of cotton wool and squeezed it hard against Squirrel's twitching nose.

"The taxidermist is fickle," Pappa said, concentrating. "He adores every subject like a lover. His hands are guided by the desire to preserve a loved one forever." I didn't like Pappa's new voice.

Squirrel's eyelids became heavier.

"Look closely, Derek," Pappa urged, "you have much to learn from life by observing death."

Pappa stopped for a moment and put a gloved hand on my shoulder. "Are you alright?"

I nodded. I didn't want to speak.

"Listen," he said, "I always sing a song, that way I feel better." It was very strange. Pappa started humming. The sound coming from his lips was familiar. It was the same tune he lulled me with when I was little, curled in bed with Jacko.

Pappa was singing Squirrel to sleep:

"Rock a bye baby, on the tree top.

When the wind blows the cradle will rock."

Squirrel closed his eyes and his legs went limp. He looked so long and thin all of a sudden. "First, I make a Ventral Incision," Pappa said. He flipped Squirrel over onto his back and slit his belly with a thin, sharp knife, pinching the skin gently between his thumb and forefinger. The skin rolled back and was red on the inside, like lips. I saw tubes and something white, like off milk, beneath the flesh.

Carefully, and quickly, Pappa worked the skin over Squirrel's leg, exposing a bulb of pink muscle. The whole leg came free with a plop.

"When the bow breaks the cradle will fall
Down will come baby, cradle and all."

Pappa peeled the pelt up to the base of Squirrel's head, like a woollen sweater pulled, inside out, off a small child.

He then freed the skin from around the ears. I couldn't stop watching. As Pappa wrenched and tugged, Squirrel swung from side to side, like a dancing puppet.

He lay Squirrel on his back and worked the pelt off his head, finally separating the skin from the body with a snip of his scissors at the nose. When I looked closer at Squirrel's nostrils, I saw blood there.

"Finished," Pappa said, satisfied. "Now to get rid of those fleas." Using a big metal spoon Pappa took different powders from jars marked SALT, ALUM, and BORAX and put them into a shallow tin bath with some water. He lay the skin, still twitching, into it. "This is called Fixing," Pappa said. I peered closer at the wet skin.

"Why is it still moving?"

"Pilo-erector muscles, under the skin," Pappa said. "It's just a nervous reaction." I didn't understand but I thought how difficult it must be to know every nerve, every bone in a squirrel's body.

I was about to say something when Pappa raised his hand to his mouth. "Ssh!" He closed his eyes and held my hand. I stood there quietly while Pappa murmured a prayer under his breath. "Done," he said and smiled at me. I was beginning to feel dizzy.

"Remember, you must love your subject," he said, patting me. "Soon it will be your turn. Not today, though. One step at a time, eh?"

I felt hot and giddy. My eyes began to close and everything started going dark. I felt myself rocking on my heels and my legs going limp.

"Derek!"

Pappa picked me up and rushed me upstairs. Before everything went dark I remember laying on the shop floor and Pappa peeling my jumper over my head the way he did when he undressed me as a boy.

He was always so good at doing that.

The next day I met Mamma and Jeffrey. Pappa dropped me off. Jeffrey was in my old anorak, holding onto Mamma's hand, like a baby. I was angry with him for having Mamma to himself. Mamma was upset and pulled me close into the folds of her coat. I didn't tell her about my faint.

The wind was blowing. There were kites above Parliament Hill. In my pocket I had some monkey nuts.

Up in a tree a Squirrel [SCIARUS VULGARIS] was

hopping along a branch. I knelt, broke the shell to powdery crumbs and held out a nut between my fingers, making sucking noises between my teeth.

Squirrel clambered down to the grass and, in short, nervous jumps, approached. He took the nut from me. In his paws it looked like a rugby ball. He crouched there on his haunches, turning the nut over and over, gnawing.

I started to hum a lullaby.

and his wife

stephanie hale

stephanie hale
was born in bromsgrove,
worcestershire, in 1966.
she has worked as a
reporter and news reader
for the bbc and independent
radio; and briefly in the
casting and drama depart-
ments at anglia television.
her poetry has been
performed at norwich
arts centre.

I STILL HAVE a fragment from the newspaper. It's been framed and nailed to the living room wall. Take a look at the picture. You might not recognise me at first. My face is in shadow, shaded by the umbrella of my husband. Now you know our names. He is Businessman John White. I am And-His- Wife. Shame it's in black and white or you might see the red glow in my eyes. Smouldering coals – seething, burning; not yet realised.

Now read the headline. It looks innocent enough: TODDLER LUCKY TO BE ALIVE. And the story. The story of how Businessman-John plunged in a river and saved a child from drowning, helped by And-His-Wife, of course.

Somehow I know my illness is rooted in this scrap of newsprint. I think the disease is word-borne in the same way that cholera is contracted through water and flu passes through the air. Microscopic bacteria flashing; flickering into my eyes and into my bloodstream. Streptococci, Gonococcus, Coccus, Bacillus. Madnuss. Invisiblenuss.

The Herald is the only clue I have. An hour after reading it, I found a thin candle of flesh between the cushions on the settee. It was slender and soft like warm white wax, the end blazing with a flame coloured finger nail. It took me a minute to realise it was a severed finger from And-His-Wife's right hand.

Sometimes I hallucinate. I see things differently. I conjure up a gusty autumn day, and two people walking beside a river. A red apple is bobbing in the water, sucked down by weeds. The apple is screaming, shouting, dying. Then I am swimming out, battling with myself and the current. Punching. Kicking. Fighting. Feet like boulders.

I grab the apple and find a boy. A drowning boy with blossom cheeks and a crimson duffle coat. A drowned boy. Dead. I grip him in my teeth and swim towards the river bank. There, others grasp the child and pump him full of life.

They thump his chest and will him to wake. He starts to leak. Weeds spew from his mouth. A new birth on the river bank. Boy-child shivering and frightened.

Then, blue flashing lights and a stomach pump; a sterile hospital ward. A thick orange tube is pushed down my throat. I stare at the rubber until my eyes cross. Mixing the words: MADE IN BRITAIN. Condensing them to: MAD IN IT.

Somewhere here, I think a mistake is made. Perhaps the nurses push the tube down the wrong hole. While I am lying there, parts of me are dripping out, slipping up the tubes and down the funnel. Into the bucket. I think I am seeing dirty river water. Instead, I am looking down at my Self.

In the months after I returned home, And-His-Wife lost various digits around the house. I found a thumb poking from her desk tidy; an index finger in her sewing basket; a middle finger sticking out of a waste-paper bin. Then there was the day when I pulled off her woollen gloves and stripped her hands bare. A clutch of fingers curled in the warmth of the gloves. Frost bite? Gangrene? I wasn't sure.

But I'm not worried by this. Diseases have cures. Perhaps And-His-Wife's fingers will grow back even-tually, like milk teeth. I am more curious than anything. The illness makes the winter months in-teresting. I distance myself and watch. I am the doctor observing the patient.

Businessman-John and And-His-Wife argued a lot about the newspaper article. She didn't like it hanging on her living room wall, even if it was in a corner.

Businessman-John didn't know what she was talk-ing about. "It's only words," he said.

"It makes me sick," said And-His-Wife. "You'd think I didn't exist at all."

"Keep your hair on," said Businessman-John. "It's not important."

After this, it was as though a mirror had shattered into a thousand pieces and one of the splinters had lodged in my eye. From then on all words looked ugly. The letters rejigged and rejumbled. They took on new meanings.

But the illness went further than the words in The Herald. I didn't take it lying down. I took it like a man and found I wasn't. I phoned the newspaper to complain.

And-His-Wife spoke to reporter David Jones. His voice was polite and well-educated. And irritated. "I wasn't there," he said. "We take our facts from the police, the ambulance, the parents."

I remembered then that no one had ever asked who she was. They had always been Mr. and Mrs. Him first, her second. It had seemed unimportant at the time. Living in Coupledom they only needed one name: like the phone book. Like the bills, the wedding invitations, the postcards from abroad.

"I am not at all happy about this," said And-His-Wife. "I saved the boy too."

The words billowed out and hung in the air like ghosts. They floated for a few seconds, hovering. Waiting.

"Sorry," said reporter David Jones. "There's nothing I can do."

And-His-Wife rang off and watched her words start to fade. First to go was the "happy". Then, slowly, the others disappeared. One by one. "I am" was the last to go. It lingered for a while, dancing just above the tip of her nose. But soon this also vanished, like mist. And-His-Wife barely blinked. It had never occurred to me before that words could be invisible.

After this, I got used to waking up and finding someone had been operating on her during the night. Amputating limbs with precise knives; stitching seams back together; leaving silver tracks where the needles had been. Already this month, I found her left arm coiled on the carpet like a broken ornament. It's in the bottom drawer of my desk now, awaiting a post mortem.

The strange thing about the illness is that no one else seems to notice. Not even Businessman-John. One evening, for a joke, And-His-Wife put her wedding finger on his dinner plate. She soaked it in vegetable stock and tucked it under a pile of mashed potatoes to see what he would do. But Businessman-John just sawed through it with his steak knife and poked it in his mouth as if it was a pork sausage.

Today starts like many others. I shut myself in the living room and pull out a battered typewriter and a folder of news cuttings. Then I cut open a thick bale of newspapers and magazines. I grab a handful from the top, and flick through, skim reading. When I see any reviews of drama productions, or profiles of actors or actresses, I snip the articles out and stick them in a scrapbook with spray-mount. This is how the PR Agency likes them.

I can't concentrate. This morning, I discovered And-His-Wife's right arm was missing. I pulled back the duvet and saw it wedged under Businessman-John. He'd rolled on to it during the night and somehow it had popped out of its socket. It was poking out under his spine, twisted in an L-shape at the elbow. I tugged it out and hid it under the bed. One day, I will have to find a cupboard for her missing bits. Perhaps she will talk to someone about false limbs. A plastic hand? A metal arm? A wooden leg?

I flick through the magazines looking at the pictures of chopped up women. Pictures of dismembered hips and lips and eyes and thighs. They all have the same symptoms of widespread mutilation. Diced and sliced and cubed like carrots. Bodiless legs straddling washing machines. Faceless lips pouting over aftershave. Headless eyes caressing coconut cookies. A general advertising massacre.

I steal other words for And-His-Wife while I scan the pages. Since the illness, I've become a word collector. Comic as a magpie. I have my own nest of names and pictures. It is interwoven with twigs and words like: LAW LORDS. NEWSMEN.

CRAFTSMEN. WEATHERMEN. WORKMEN. CAMERAMEN. AD MEN. AMBULANCEMEN. LANDLORDS. SECURITY MEN. MILKMEN. POSTMASTERS. SPOKESMEN. CHAIRMEN. AIRMEN. TAX MEN. CUSTOMS MEN. FROG-MEN. Sometimes the newsprint is attached to photographs of women. Usually it is linked to other words. I give these to And-His-Wife as medicine, knowing somehow they feed the disease, but believing they will also cure it. I once saved thirty And-His-Wifes for her in one day. But after about a week I gave up collecting namesakes. There were too many of them.

I work for several hours until my spine starts to ache. I feel sick and dizzy. It could be fumes from the glue or just the way I've been sitting, but my head hurts. I open my mouth and feel a tell-tale clicking. I move my tongue from side to side and feel it pulling at the roots.

"Not my speech," I think. "Not her thoughts."

"Not my thoughts."

It is time to shelve amateur medicine and call in the experts. At two-thirty, And-His-Wife pulls a winter coat over my invisible arms and takes a bus to the health centre.

"It's an emergency," she says. "I have to see a doctor."

The receptionist is distracted by the buzzing of telephones and a man in a white coat pointing at a kettle.

Her head swivels like an owl's. She snatches up a receiver, pulls a jar of Nescafé out of her drawer, and pencils in an appointment.

"Take a seat Mrs. White," she says. Her chin grips the telephone, turning her smile into a grimace.

And-His-Wife sits in the waiting room until her number is called, then finds her way along the corridors to Doctor Peter Evans. She knocks and enters. He is sipping a cup of steaming black coffee. And-His-Wife sits on the edge of a stiff black vinyl chair and shakes her head. She starts to cry.

"What can we do for you today?" asks Doctor Peter Evans. He hands over a Kleenex tissue; a large white truce flag.

"Who am I?" she asks. "I don't even know my name."

And-His-Wife starts to tell him about the invisible money she earns. The unnoticed meals. The unseen dust she wipes from furniture. The mysterious weeds which vanish from the flowerbeds.

Doctor Peter Evans puts his finger to his lips. Then he sighs, turns away, and taps some notes on his computer keyboard. The screen reflects his face and I can see him biting his lip. He is not surprised. He thinks it is genetic. A disease passed down from And-His-Wife's mother and her mother's mother before her. A mutant X-chromosome And-His-Wife should carry like a cross. He has no cure. Only forgetfulness.

"Have you ever considered tranquillisers?" he asks.

"They might help."
Doctor Peter Evans prints out a slip of white paper.
Valium.
"Come back and see me in a week," he says.

And-His-Wife leaves the surgery and walks straight past the chemists. I am sure now that the disease is terminal. Neither pills nor potions can save me. When I get home I put the prescription in my file of words. Valium is a different type of word from the others, but I'm sure it is connected.

I climb the stairs to my bedroom. I feel a tremendous tiredness now. My feet are heavy and my eyelids swollen. And-His-Wife pulls off my jeans and sweater and finds my chest and stomach missing. She can see straight through my middle, see the elegant skeleton of the chair behind me. Only my legs and head remain, held together by a transparent thread. And-His-Wife is not sure where my centre has gone. Perhaps I left it on the bus? It'll be in lost property. The torso wedged between dusty umbrellas and broken shopping baskets.

I am too tired to care. I slip between the sheets and float there, skinny dipping, letting sleep wash over me. No apples here. No drownings. I turn over and do the backstroke, pushing out to sea. Arm over arm. Legs kicking, slip-slapping with the waves. Leaping towards the wan face of the afternoon moon.

And-His-Wife is still asleep when Businessman-John arrives home; her back arched like a sea horse; her toes curled like whelks.

"Don't forget we're going out for a meal tonight," he says, tugging at a strand of long seaweed hair.

He reaches into the water and strokes her thighs; kisses my invisible breasts.

"Do we have to go?" asks And-His-Wife.

But Businessman-John is already fumbling in the wardrobe for a tie.

And-His-Wife dries off and puts on a sleek black dress to disguise the hole in my stomach. She pulls black lace gloves over my armless arms. Fortunately, I still have feet for the patent leather shoes.

"You look stunning," says Businessman-John.

He doesn't seem to notice bits of me are missing.

We take a taxi to the restaurant. The menu is elaborate: Kiwi fruit and goats cheese; asparagus puffs; cream cheese and broccoli croustade; banana flambé with honey sauce; almond biscuit baskets. The waitress arrives and looks at Businessman-John for the order. But he's not playing. He lets And-His-Wife pick her own meal. These small things are important to her now.

But no one tells the waitress. She goes to the bar and brings back a wine list which she hands to Businessman-John. So the forgetfulness is passed on like a Chinese Whisper. And-His-Wife's husband pushes back the leather-bound cover and peruses the names. Choosing the words. He-words. It's traditional. Some rules are not meant to be broken. Businessman-John selects a Chateau Pech-Celeyran.

"Excuse me!" says And-His-Wife. "I'm paying for the meal too."

The waitress looks at her and looks away again. I'm not sure if she's seen me. Perhaps she is staring at an empty chair.

"Your order, Sir?" she says. Then she scribbles on her note pad and hurries away.

"What's wrong with you?" asks Businessman-John. "Get a grip."

"Women don't get a grip," I say. "They lose control. It's traditional."

The waitress returns with a bottle, tucked in a silver cooler like a funeral casket. She displays the wine label and pulls out the corkscrew with an expert twist. She flicks the serviette out of Businessman-John's glass and pours the wine. I watch from a distance while he sniffs, looks for cork, then swills the liquid around his mouth. He nods smugly. Then the waitress pours liquid in And-His-Wife's glass. She avoids my eyes.

"Cheers!" says Businessman-John. "Here's to us!"

He leans forward to chink glasses. But instead, my invisible arms tilt and hit the bottle of Chateau Pech-Celeyran. It tips over in slow motion. Liquid spreads across the table.

"God!" gasps her husband. "God!"

The wine is already seeping into the table cloth, into Businessman-John's lap. His shirt is stained crimson. His trousers are damp. His face is also wet. In this light, the wine looks like blood. Pale and congealing.

Then there is a flash of serviettes and white granules. Salt is scattered in his wounds.

"That should get it out," the waitress says.

"I think we'd better go home," says And-His-Wife's husband.

There are no cabs. There is a football match on the other side of the city; the taxi rank is still and quiet.

"Let's take the bus," says And-His-Wife.

Her husband holds back.

"I'll phone for a cab," he says. "Wait here!"

But And-His-Wife is already striding on without him.

"Wait for me!" shouts her husband.

And-His-Wife marches ahead. She is exhilarated. Intoxicated. Drunk on the January air and her own sense of change.

And-His-Wife's husband quickens his pace. I hear his breath before I see him in the darkness. He is just a shadow.

"What are you playing at!" he shouts.

He is striding into the light towards And-His-Wife.

"Why can't you act normal?" he pleads. "Just this once."

He is near her now. I can see his teeth and the glint of his belt buckle.

And-His-Wife stares at the floor for inspiration.

"Don't look now but my legs have disappeared," I say.

Somehow they have detached themselves in the restaurant. They tumbled to the floor as I made my exit. This is something new. Two limbs snapping off at once. But And-His-Wife feels no fear, only a sense of the inevitable. A giddiness of spirit. She is now a head wearing a dress. On invisible stilts, swaying in the wind. Unbalanced. Unsteady. Unstable.

"What is it like down there?" she asks.

"What are you on?" asks her husband.

His voice is faint and distant, as if it's crackling through headphones. Static. Something has happened to And-His-Wife's ears.

The Number 3 bus arrives. And-His-Wife climbs up the step and her husband has no choice but to follow. It is packed with football supporters waving black and white scarves and shouting slogans. And-His-Wife finds a seat at the rear. Her husband tiptoes through the thicket of legs. He is furious.

"I'll never be able to show my face in that restaurant again!" he says.

He squashes up against the window. He can't bring himself to touch me. The joyous Me hovering above the seat.

The bus conductor comes by, clicking his ticket machine. He touches his cap and asks my husband for the fare. Instead, And-His-Wife reaches into her invisible purse and pulls out a fiver. He doesn't take any notice of her floating head; just tears off the tickets and hands them back while her husband glares.

I have a new prognosis for the illness now. It is not deadly; not cancerous. On the contrary, our arms and fingers have only just started to grow. We are a rose bush: constantly being pruned and sending out new shoots. A life-cycle of lush green leaves and snapped stems.

My thoughts are broken by the tiger's cry of a baby. I look up into the desperate tired eyes of a young mother. The screams are louder than words; words louder than thoughts. A man holding a crocheted white shawl sits near the mother and baby. Near enough, but far away. Dissociating himself.

"I wish we'd taken a taxi," says my husband bitterly.

The baby screams the plaintive wail of tea-time. The woman looks down so she doesn't have to meet our eyes. She tries poking her finger in the baby's mouth, pretending it's a nipple. I watch her breasts leaking on to her blouse. Damp circles spreading outwards. The woman's nails dig into her hands like thorns. She is wishing herself invisible.

"I wish she'd shut that brat up," says my husband loudly.

I feel a furnace spark into life. Quick flames flash

through my intestines. Roaring. If I open my mouth, my tongue will scorch.

The bus pulls to a halt. The woman with the baby stands up. She struggles down the gangway with her pushchair, hooking the child over her shoulder. The father waits, then follows in her wake. He mouths something, but the woman can't hear it above the football chants. Her face is blank. The family steps off the bus.

Then, thump! A skull drops down from mid-air. Bouncing off the seat on to the floor. Somersaulting down the aisle past the conductor. Then bump, bump, bump, down the steps. Jumping onto the street and into the woman's shoulder bag. The doors wheeze shut. Sighing.

I look out as we drive away. And-His-Wife's head stares back, briefly. Her face is sad, but her eyes are smiling.

"Good riddance," says my husband. "I thought we'd never see the back of her."

"Not we," I say. "You."

We glare at each other. Then there is a sudden rush of air; an uplifting whoosh! And I am no longer touching the earth. I am flying. Gliding. Snaring the clouds. I look out to where my arms were. I see wings.

extract from

an invisible woman

n v k baylis

nvk baylis went to st
albans school and exeter
university, graduating in
psychology in 1988 and
going on to research in
criminology. making a living
has led to many things,
including work in an
approved school, lecturing
evening classes in
psychopathology, and
running a prison writing
group. having lived and
travelled throughout north
america, the author recently
befriended the city of san
francisco. interests are
novel and film.

NOWHERE VERY special on New Year's Eve.

Another feeble party, just a little too far from San Francisco. Susan had been knocking back the nuts and raisins and what was left of the booze. And why not? No one had warned her who was coming. They probably thought it'd be funny: the shame on her face, the shock on his. After all, they hadn't seen each other for the past ten years. Susan had been so careful to avoid anyone who might recall her teenage years, anyone who might smirk at what she'd become—or rather, what she hadn't.

She might have sensed what was just about to happen. The silver metal tree blinked and blinked its warning. An electronic Father Christmas cackled ho-ho-ho in expectation. The front door opened.

Susan ceased to breathe when she heard a familiar voice greeting people. She turned and saw him: he'd never worn spectacles but here they were now. His

eyes hunted the room through heavy, round, tor-
toiseshell frames. Quick as she could, she slipped into
the next room, and thought she'd gotten away with it,
too, when a voice bellowed, "Susan!"

Her body damp with panic, she turned, expecting
to be met with a look of horror. Yet all she saw was
Toby's wide, welcome smile. Grinning, he made such
an awful fuss of her, hugging her tight into his arms.
God, he smelt good. She couldn't help but hug him
back. Closing her eyes against all the stares, she held
him, felt his muscles bunching beneath his cashmere
jacket.

It could have been worse, thought Susan. She could
have been relegated from one-time lover to the level
of old friend: asked to shake the hand she'd once
held, asked to kiss the face she'd once made cry. Even
so, she knew it was going to hurt, to talk about the
weather when once there were storms inside.

Toby stepped back and began explaining just how
it was he'd found her. A guy she worked with at the
West Oakland youth club...

Susan wasn't listening. She was thinking back to
when they were fourteen years old and she'd first met
Tobias Bellini. He'd offered her a lift on his bicycle
and she'd perched on the saddle, holding on to his
dancing hips. Later, they stood panting amid the trees
of a favourite park. There, his fingertips had brought
Susan to her first orgasm.

Toby had been good looking even then, or cute at

least: a hungry adolescent. And now? Now he looked as lean and powerful as a middleweight boxer. He'd had his teeth done, though, like a cupboard of best china, white and even against the taut, brown skin of his face.

Susan interrupted him mid-sentence. "Your shirts ironed! You're not married, are you? You and Bambi over there?" and she nodded toward the woman who had wafted in behind him and been instantly engulfed in a slick of oily men.

Toby looked amused. "Married to Katrina? No, no."

A ribbed top and rounded bottom, was that what he went for? Then what did he want with Susan after all these years? She glanced sideways to a mirror and cringed at her own reflection. How very seasonal, she mused; with all that make-up on such a round, white face, anyone would think she'd come as a Christmas cake, iced and inedible. Around her chin, painful lumps threatened to erupt in celebration.

It was no surprise to Susan that Toby was somewhat shocked. Oh, he tried well enough to hide it, but he'd looked a little too long and wide-eyed at her bulk beneath the lime green tent. Her shoes were scuffed, her dress was stained; it would seem she'd let herself go. He was so tall and broad, so beautifully dressed. She was bursting with a serious question, but knew she had to make light of it.

"Come on then, Tobes, tell me where your life went wrong?"

He shrugged bashfully. "I went into art."

"Art! Hold on there, mister, the last thing I recall, you ran off to join the Marines."

He nodded. "And five years on, I crawled back out."

Susan noticed how slowly and deliberately Toby spoke, as if he was used to being listened to. Her own voice seemed loud and fast in comparison. "So what d'ya do now, Picasso? Paint?"

"No, no. I'm a dealer."

Susan whistled in a show of awe. "Wow! Oh, but I should've guessed it. Bambi's the very picture of beauty. Must have cost you a mint."

She couldn't believe what she'd just said and swung the conversation round to avoid his reply. "Oh, and are you still... still an old movie nut?" He'd once collected glossy pin-ups and taken her to the pictures all the time.

To her relief, Toby grinned like a cheeky schoolboy, though she couldn't think why. "I guess you'd say modern classics are more my cup of tea."

She mocked him with an upper class English accent. "Oh, so we're drinking tea now, are we?" She dropped it just as quickly. "And where do you work, Tobes? In the City?"

"Sometimes, and sometimes back in New York. You see, I've got these little galleries I like to go between."

Susan's mouth fell open. He was Bellini? *Bellini's of San Francisco?* She'd walked by once or twice, but never thought in a million years...

It was the sort of place where they frisked you at the door and then gave you champagne in a vase. It was all too much for Susan and she began to laugh. There was Toby, the dashing playboy who'd made his fortune in international art. And here was Susan, also dashing—dashing around as an overweight and underpaid office worker, tired of her life but scared of losing her job.

Toby didn't see the joke and could only manage a baffled smile. Had he lost his sense of humour, Susan wondered. Laughter, too often, only looked like happiness. Perhaps he'd found the real thing and no longer had to be funny.

"Sorry, Tobes, it's just that I'm rather shocked and... and proud of you. Proud we were friends."

He looked hurt by this, as if to say 'Still are, aren't we?' but he didn't miss the chance to ask, "What about Susan? What have you been doing, since you stopped talking back through those braces?"

She got in quick with, "Heard anything about the rest of that crowd?"

He paused but let her get away with it, and rattled off some dusty names. Teresa, Ruth, and Felicity had either become lawyers or married them, whichever paid more. Susan rolled her eyes.

Kate Thompson had become a teacher and been in and out of mental homes. Susan should have guessed it. Her homework was far too neat. What she hadn't guessed was that Thelma was dying of cancer and John Row had been killed in a bike accident. Those two had been worth a hundred of the others. She wanted to ask more, but Toby wouldn't give up. "Still haven't heard what became of Susan Lock?"

And Susan hoped to God that no one had. She could just imagine the coffee-table gossip. 'You'd never believe it about old Lockers! She's huge now, apparently, and a typist or something dreadful.'

She hoped they thought she was dead. But it wasn't only being fat that she felt ashamed about. The thing was, she'd done absolutely nothing with all those years since high school. That, in itself, was an incredible achievement, now she came to think of it. How could anyone live so long and do so little? Become obese yet disappear?

She desperately wanted to tell him the truth, to burst into sobs on Toby's shoulder and let him in on her past. She gulped her drink, once, twice, and looking anywhere but at Toby, began: "All told, my last ten years have been rather more shocking than impressive. When I took off kinda' quickly like I did, I planned to live by my wits... until I realised I didn't have any. So I just sort of drifted around the place for five years, and then I drifted back."

Susan was impressed at how couldn't-care-less she'd made her voice sound.

"And what are you now?" Toby wanted to know.

She screwed her face into a mock frown. "Me?" She

stared into her dry martini. "I'm a pumpkin waiting to become a princess." She looked at her digital watch. 11:33.

She glanced back up and realised Toby wasn't looking at her. He seemed suddenly irritated, uncomfortable with the noise of people screeching drunkenly at each other's jokes. As he looked around, Susan took a peek through those imposing new glasses. Whyever else he wore them, it wasn't to see any better. Those lenses didn't change a thing.

"What am I now?" she repeated mechanically as he turned back to face her. Toby probably already knew, but there was no way Susan was going to admit to him that she worked in the office of a chewing gum factory. She forced out a phony chuckle. "Well, when you're this close to thirty, having done so little, a word like 'loser' comes to mind."

"No, it doesn't," he told her. "You're only a loser if you give up trying. Until then you're still armed and dangerous."

She only huffed. "Oh, I'm dangerous alright, Tobes. I get into an elevator... and everyone sweats."

"Bullshit, Susan. You're a late bloomer, that's all."

Jokes she could handle; it was the kind lines that hurt. But Susan smiled and really meant it. She was half relieved, half ashamed to see her best and oldest friend. She didn't know whether to hug him again, or tear out of the room in tears. Finally, she compromised and told him she had to be going.

Damn it, he offered to drive her. She was about to explain that her own car was parked around the block, but thought better of it. He'd only ask to walk her outside, and then he'd witness the rusting heap that probably wouldn't start. Better say she was going by cab. But then she wasn't sure she had the fare. Oh, stuff it, she'd let Tobes drive her. It'd only take a minute and then the whole ugly thing would be over. Katrina's jaw tightened when Toby informed her he was running his old pal home. She'd tried to look wounded, but Toby hadn't waited to register her pout of disapproval. He'd simply strode off across the room to apologise to the host. Until then, Katrina had been quite happy among that shoal of gawpers whom she'd humiliated with her dimpled smirk. Without anything to say for herself, she'd smoked and pushed her hair behind her ear countless times. At the news of Toby's imminent departure, she abandoned her groupies without so much as a nod, and came straight over to Susan. Her highly polished tone suggested she'd over-rehearsed. "I take it you're the infamous Suzie?"

Oh dear! thought Susan. Bambi's jealous. Slender and platinum blonde, with a face as irresistible as any kitten's, yet still she glowed emerald green.

"I'm Susan, if that's what you mean."

Her calmness only riled Katrina more, who retorted, "Tibbs said you'd be here and went on and on about you. But I must say, I'd never have known you

from his description. Was it quite some time ago?"
Tibbs?

Ah, yes. That would be Katrina's pillow-name for
Toby, so everyone would know things were 'special'.

Don't worry, thought Susan, we all assume he
humps you. Then before she could help herself,
Susan said, "I didn't think even Toby would recognise
me. You see, I've been ill for some time. The drugs
have made things... difficult."

Katrina looked suitably embarrassed, and even
Susan winced at her own dreadful lie. Oh, what the
hell, at least it shut the brat up. Somewhat ironic, too,
when Susan considered how she was indeed dying—
from chronic boredom and malignant shame. It was
nothing that couldn't be cured by the simple injec-
tion of a speeding bullet into her booze-muddled
brain.

In the nick of time, Toby returned, and she and
Bambi said "B'bye" with all the instant warmth of a
microwave oven. Out in the drizzle and the empty
Oakland streets, Susan barely noticed the orange
glow in the western sky. San Francisco in New Year's
celebration. Her mind wandered back to the five
years when she and Toby had gone out, boyfriend
and girlfriend, upstairs Friday nights with their under-
wear down. Mom would come in with the supper
tray to find their orgasm-flushed faces intently reading Shakespeare.

"Susan?"

Toby was calling her back. Only now did she realise she'd walked on without him. He was starting the engine of a low, black car. The smell of exhaust in the night air was comfort against the winter cold. With a purr, the headlights opened out of the bonnet, like eyelids, and shot a look of light some fifty yards in front.

When they were sixteen, they'd spent all their allowance on bus fares, but Toby had always sworn he'd have one of these. And now here was Susan, cushioned by the plush, scented leather. It was spotless. She curled her fingers to hide the ragged nails. At least she'd worn her 'new' overcoat, the one she'd gotten five years ago.

They drove across town, Toby's face saddening as the streets grew more sleazy. People slept huddled in the doorways of liquor stores and adult shows. "I'm surprised you live so close to your mom's old place."

"It's only temporary," she told him.

"So's life, Susan."

She huffed. "Oh, I'll get the hang of growing up... next time around," but her false smile faded as she spied two lovers walking arm in arm.

They drew up outside a tired, little house and sat with the silence and the thumping heartbeat of the windscreen wipers. Toby spoke first. "Why did you stay away so long? Everyone said you were dead."

She wanted to say, 'I am dead, Toby, can't you tell?', but went for second best. "It took you ten years to come and find me, you obviously believed them."

"I was counting on you, Susan. I felt you let me down."

She sneered. "Oh, poor old Toby. Must have been awful struggling on as an Officer Marine and a multi-millionaire."

A clock began to toll and Toby squinted through the glass, as if looking for the sound. "There's the side you see and the side you don't." He looked back at her to say, "You're the only one who really knows how things were. We were good for each other, you and me. Quite a team. Remember?"

Susan swallowed. "Yes, quite a team. And now?"

These thoughts had been seething inside her since the moment they'd met, and they surfaced uncontrollably. "Now I'm a fat joke, I'm all but thirty, I work fifty hours a week. And you know what? I wonder why I bother. Not a lot you can say to that, is there, Tobes? You with your money and your..."

"I don't think you're a fat joke, Susan. I doubt your life is all that funny. And the only thing I wonder is, why?"

Susan stared into her lap, letting the tears fall onto her hands rather than roll down her face. "Things didn't go according to plan. Remember those fabulous plans we made, lying in the dark?"

He nodded. "So what became of the wonderful lives we were always going to lead?"

And before she could stop herself, Susan had

replied, "God knows, Toby. I hope this isn't me."

He gave a tired sigh. "If only you hadn't run off."

"I'd lost all reason to stay."

Toby turned toward her angrily. "No, no, no. I was nineteen... nobody... broke. I had to go away. Had to be someone special so..." and he looked the other way, out the window. "So Susan Lock could marry me."

Lights flashed in the house across the road; people were cheering. Susan scrambled out of the car and made for the darkness of her front door. She dashed inside, slumping against the closed door, hit by the words he'd shouted through the rain:

"What ever happened to you—and the woman you wanted to be?"

the effigy

jacqui lofthouse

jacqui lofthouse worked for four years as a radio producer. she produced the first independently made programme to be broadcast on the world service, the first drink-drive radio advertising campaign, and an aids radio campaign in six languages. she has also worked extensively in media training, teaching television and radio interview skills, and has toured southern india as an actress. jacqui has completed her first novel, *the age of the fish,* and is currently working on her second, *the temple of hymen,* about an eighteenth century sex therapist.

On January 19th 1729, the dramatist William Congreve died. He bequeathed his estate to his mistress, the Duchess of Marlborough. In order to minimize gossip, he made her husband, Francis, second Earl of Godolphin, executor.

As it was widely believed that Congreve's relationship with the Duchess had been platonic, the will seemed eccentric. But the Duchess grieved openly for Congreve, and as a result many stories circulated about their relationship. Some said that she secured a life-sized waxen statue of him which she worshipped or treated in an unnatural way.

YOU SPEAK to me, Madam, but you do not hear my voice. Each day since the funeral, I have been with you, and at night in your bed-chamber I watch you sleep. I try not to look at Godolphin. His presence disturbs me, more than you may imagine.

I was a man of wit, dear Henrietta, but what am I now, without my tongue or my pen? My words are nothing but self-pity and vexation. Because I have neither the luxury of an audience nor the comfort of friends, I am at liberty to express myself as I please. For the first time, I am not obliged to be charming.

Yesterday, once again, you had the physician attend to my gout. He unravelled the bandages that swathe my feet, prodded the afflicted area, shook his head grimly and wrapped me in fresh dressings. Then he looked at my eyes and, seeing no improvement, said he could do nothing for my cataracts. Foolish man! Does he not recognize that I am no longer blind? I see very clearly now. Nothing escapes me.

They have heard about me in the town, it seems. Did you believe that you could keep this to yourself? It is all rumour, of course. Nothing that can be substantiated. I trust you have paid your servants handsomely to remain discreet. Yet the word has spread. They talk of me at Drury Lane and in the chocolate houses. "Mr. Congreve lives!" they laugh. "He has risen from the grave and is alive and well in St. James' with the Duchess of Marlborough."

Did you not think of my reputation, Henrietta, when you thought to breathe life into me? Do you think that any man, however great his fame, can survive this ridicule? Hear me, my love; do not gaze at your reflection. Will it always be thus? That I am here to comfort you when you grieve for me, but when I wish to speak you will deny my existence. Am I to be your doll and nothing more?

Lady, you invented me. I did not ask to live beyond the grave. I certainly did not wish to be resurrected in St. James'. Take me to Wills to see Pope and Berkeley. Perhaps they will rejoice to see their friend returned from the dead.

Ah, you turn toward me now, disarming me with your beauty, and I can no longer rail. You put your hands to your hair, releasing the pins that hold it. It falls around your shoulders, pale chestnut red. I do not believe I have ever seen you look so lovely. Who would have thought it? That the dead man sees better than the living. Even before my eyes deteriorated, when we both were younger, you did not have this air of naturalness. You do not truly believe I am here, my love, I understand that now. You do not know that I watch you, and so you have no art. I have never seen a woman without art. Even Mrs. Bracegirdle... I apologize... but you do not hear me, so why should I not speak of my former love? Ann Bracegirdle could have been my wife; but a gentleman cannot marry an actress. And Arabella, my singing Angel. She made every place alike heavenly. I had thought to meet her again in Heaven, but it was not to be. You have arrested my journey there.

I try to understand you, Henrietta, but my heart overflows. You did this because you love me, because you cannot bear to part with me. And yet... was it also to taunt the Earl, your husband? Could you not let him be, dear Godolphin, dull as he is, and give the last years of your life to him? Is my Duchess so spiteful as to wish him eternal cuckoldom?

When I died, you could not bear to let me go. My soul desired to meet the Almighty, but your grief was too much. I could not desert you in your hour of need. I thought my funeral would release me. It was not the funeral I requested, but I forgave you even that. A quiet occasion, I had said, without the least ostentation. But you had me buried as if I were your Duke, in the nave of Westminster Abbey; in your family plot, so that you may join me hereafter. I felt myself carried above the heads of Bridgewater, Cobham, Godolphin, and Wilmington. It was not a fitting end. But soon, I thought, there would be silence. Yes, in those final moments, before my soul departed, I had doubts. I was afraid that all our human hopes may be but dreams; ephemera. Vain creatures to trust that we will be saved and not just returned to dust.

Don't look at me so, Henrietta. That dummy you stare on is not me. A waxen effigy indeed! You stroke its wig - how touching. But it is not me, I tell you. Your dabbling has brought me back, but I do not reside in that ridiculous figure, though I reside with it. Does it look like Congreve, the greatest Comic Dramatist of the age?

Do I boast? A dead man must be allowed some pleasures. I could have called myself the greatest Tragedian also. Do you remember? 'Heaven has no rage, like love to hatred turned.' You used to say that

Mrs. Bracegirdle was the woman of whom I wrote.
'Nor hell a fury like a woman scorned.' You liked to
mock her.

"William, shall we go through to the dining-room?"
Ha! You speak.
"I believe Joseph has prepared Quail and Partridge. Will you
sup this evening?"
Madam, I come from the spirit world. Would you
have me be corporeal?
"I shall ask Francis to carry you. You are too weak to walk. Oh,
that fool Arbuthnot, why can he not cure your gout?"
I would walk, I assure you, if I could, my love. But
lately I have discovered that I prefer to float.
"Let me look at you, William."
Look at a dummy, Madam. The man himself has
gone.
"Perhaps I should powder your nose?"
I have no nose, Henrietta! Have you lost your
senses? I cannot believe that this is the woman I loved.
What? You apply rouge to the monster? You kiss its
forehead? Horrible.
"Have I made you too like a fop, Sir? I hope not. I would you
were a Mirabell and not a Witwoud."
Me? A Witwoud? This is too much. If I am a
Witwoud, I would call you Lady Wishfort. You would
not like that, my dear. No, you must stop this nonsense. My plays are for the stage, not for your bed-
chamber. You should not make a fop of me after my

death. I was ever a man of fashion and good manners. An indolent man perhaps, a disappointed man, in spite of my fame. But never a fop.

"Ah, Francis. Where have you been? Poor William's gout is bad. Could you carry him through to the dining-room?"

"Yes, my love. Of course."

What kind of a man is this, who will bear this waxy burden? Can you call him a husband? A man who secured his office only through marriage and attends the House of Lords only in order to sleep.

How the servants snigger at the sight; a husband, bowing beneath the weight of his dead rival. His horns should grow excessive long now.

"Where should I set him down, Henrietta?"

"In his usual place, Sir. I am surprised that you ask."

Could it be, Duchess, that he wants me gone? Or that he hopes you will set the fat doll in a corner, out of his sight?

"Would Mr. Congreve like potatoes?"

"Yes, Mrs. Waters."

Do you not think it strange, love, that they question nothing? They allow you to speak for me. Do you not wonder what they make of it?

"Can you fill Mr. Congreve's glass, Tom?"

And what must young Mary think? I see it in her eyes. My mother has gone mad! It does not escape her, in spite of her tender years. Even Godolphin seems different today. He is brooding.

"Why are you silent, Francis? Is the meal not to your liking?"

You see it also. But perhaps you should not ask.

"I was thinking of the will, my love."

"Yes, Francis."

"The whole town is talking of it."

"His was indeed an unusual bequest."

"That he should leave his estate to you?"

"I cannot imagine what he was thinking of."

"They say that he had a great many poor relations, and some say a son by Mrs. Bracegirdle."

"Sir, I will not have you defame him. Mary, have you finished your meal sweet heart? Good. Mrs. Waters, could you take Mary to the nursery?"

Mrs. Bracegirdle indeed. That he could think of it and not look closer to home.

"And that you should squander the money so!"

"I am a rich woman, Francis. I have put aside three thousand pounds for Mary. What else should I do with the remainder?"

"I do not presume to tell you that, my love. But that you should frivol away seven thousand pounds."

"You think my necklace and earrings extravagant?"

"Yes, dear. I do."

"And do you not find my jewels becoming?"

"I have not seen you wear them, Henrietta, but I do not think that even Mr. Congreve here would approve of your improvidence."

"Perhaps we should ask him. Mr. Congreve, Sir. Do you think me reckless for spending your legacy on diamonds?"

My love, I have seen you wear the diamonds. I have

seen them scatter light about your face and neck. And can you ask me this? I was transported, Henrietta. Their mineral glow catching on your apricot flesh. The candles burned dimly, they were down to the very stubs. And I was not angry then. I did not ask to be released, because my Heaven was in your eyes. The diamonds become you, love. At the heart of a diamond lies a star, so in that necklace is our little universe.

"He does not reply, Madam. Could it be that Mr. Congreve has lost his tongue?"

"Francis. I beg you. Mr. Congreve is exceedingly ill."

"And pray, what is that disease whereby one loses one's ability to speak?"

"He has not lost his speech, Sir, he merely rests."

"Well might such a corpulent man deserve his rest."

This is outrageous. He never dared mock my figure whilst I lived.

"I cannot listen to you, Francis."

"Perhaps it is time you did listen, Henrietta. Mr. Congreve, I fear, lives no more. Mr. Congreve, Madam, is in his grave."

I had not imagined the good man could be so bold. He should have come to this before now. My Duchess rises. She colours. She stammers.

"Sir, you... I have not... it cannot... you offend our guest. Pray..."

I see the tears form, jewel-like, in her eyes. Godolphin suffers to see her so. His remorse is apparent but he cannot reclaim his words.

"Pray, sir. Leave us alone."

"No, love, let us sit down."

"If you will not leave us, Francis, I shall retire to my chamber."

Is she to leave me here with him? This is not kind of her. But she turns and exits without looking behind.

"So, Mr. Congreve! It is time that you and I entered upon a discussion, man to man."

Man to spirit, rather, you should say.

"What, Sir, do you propose I do now?"

Why do you ask me? The worms are at me, Godolphin. They gnaw my brain.

"What do you make of her strange attachment to you?"

More than even you divine, Sir.

"I have made a mistake this evening, that much is certain. Yet should she always triumph over me in this manner? Am I to have no respect?"

Sir, you are as mad as she to address a dummy. And you will never gain her respect.

"Nobody doubts that she was faithful to me, William. They are puzzled by the will. You were indeed a good companion to her, but why should she construct this 'thing'. It is more ugly than the original, if that is indeed possible."

Worse and worse. And yet, Sir, not so ugly that I could not cuckold you.

"Methinks the man himself was fatter still."

You loved me in life, Francis. Oh, that her tampering should come to this.

"If I could only know the truth!"

The truth is worse. It will burn your heart away.

You do not listen? You turn to the fire. But I will tell my tale, for if I do not speak, I cannot rest.

After death, Francis, all is not simple. I imagined that when release finally came, the decisions made in my lifetime would seem clearer; that I would see the error of my ways. Before I met Henrietta, I thought of myself as a moral man.

'From hence let those be warned, who mean to wed;

Lest mutual falsehood stain the bridal-bed:
For each deceiver to his cost may find,
That marriage frauds too oft are paid in kind.'

Yet I could not live according to my words. And I love Henrietta still. Wife, husband, it comes to nought. It is only love that has substance.

I am evasive. I delay the truth. But the truth, Sir, is the fact that you always denied. Your daughter is not your daughter. You do not start? How you would if you could hear. She was conceived in an adulterous bed. We made the beast with two backs, Francis. We were prime as goats, as hot as monkeys, as salt as wolves in pride. Is this the candour you require? Your Mary is not your Mary, nor has she ever been. Does your green-eyed monster rage now? Moll Congreve they christened her once, but you did not believe them. You saw her plainness and knew her to be a Godolphin.

And am I proud of my success? That all the town talks of the oddity of my will yet none suspects me? It was a clever turn that, to make you the executor. It removes suspicion. And so, all my property, my envied books, my portrait, my plate, my diamond ring, all will go, eventually, to Mary. And if you were to look closer at the famed diamond necklace, you would see how my initials are carved upon the back of every collet. So when Mary inherits that, she will carry me with her, all her life. I admit, I did not play fairly. But I love your wife.

"Sir, my lady desires to see Mr. Congreve."

"Alright, Tom. Tell her Mr. Congreve seems to have recovered. She can wait on him here. I will retire to the library."

Alone now; waiting for my Henrietta. Will she come with a light step or will she rail and frown? Alas, she has suffered for me, and yet I think I have the greater complaint. Oh, this loneliness is overbearing. How long can I continue thus? Another week? A month? A year? I would not be immortal long. It pains me to see Henrietta's grief. She does not show it; she smiles on the effigy as if it were me, and yet I see by the cast of her eye that she is not deceived. She is delaying her pain. And so long as my image remains, she will continue to suspend her sorrow.

Indeed, I guess right. For here she comes, all lugubrious.

"William, my dear. I have been thinking. How can I express what has passed through my mind?"

Easier than I can, Henrietta, that much is certain.

Take your fingers from the waxy face. It may melt
beneath their heat.

"I have been thinking on Francis' words and I know them to
be true. You do not live Mr. Congreve. I have been deluded."

I do not live-no indeed-and yet I do exist.

"But though I know these heavy eyes, these fine brows, to be
but wax and horse-hair, I feel you here my love. I feel you with
me."

She sits in the lap of the dummy and kisses its ashen
face. It is more than I can bear.

"Can you remember, William, when my brother died of the
small-pox? You did not know me then, yet in your poem, I became Amaryllis, my brother, the Marquis, became Amyntas. It
made me love you. You pitied me, though you had never seen
my face.

'Tell me, thou Sun that round the world dost shine,

Hast thou beheld another Loss like mine?'

It was a great loss indeed; I felt that I should never recover. Yet
this is greater. My grief o'ershadows any sentiment I ever felt before. Oh, William, it is as if my heart is being crushed."

My Henrietta. I cannot mock you now. I cannot
leave you neither.

"I had a mother once. I loved her and yet she could not understand me. I remember when I first became acquainted with you
and your friends from the Kit-Kat Club. She did not like that. I
had lost all shame, she said, and the company I kept was corrupt-
ing my morals. And so we became estranged. I lost my mother,
William, but I gained your love."

I am not proud of that. You have not always treated

the old Duchess as you ought.

"Shall we go to the bed-chamber? I cannot lose you yet. You must stay with me for a while. Tom! Where is that wretched boy? Tom! Ah. Could you bring Mr. Congreve through to my chamber?"

"Yes, Ma'am."

My Duchess walks ahead, the thick silk of her skirts skimming the passage-way. I see her reflected endlessly in the mirrored walls. Her step is sombre. How heavy it is to be mortal.

Behind her, Tom struggles with my figure.

"What are you doing, child? Hold Mr. Congreve steady."

What's this?

"Don't drop it, Tom. Hold on!"

"I can't, Ma'am. I can't keep hold of it."

I am dazzled, Henrietta. I feel as though I see, suddenly, through the eyes of the effigy. I am hurtling toward the glass. My head clashes against silver, and shards of brilliant light shatter around me, a million broken pieces. But it is not just the mirror that is splintering. It is I, Henrietta. Your doll has broken.

"William!"

I am still here, my love. I see the effigy; pieces scattering across the floor. An arm is in three parts; the head has rolled clean off. You cannot speak. You stare at the bloodless carnage. And I too am affected. I cannot stay, Henrietta. I feel myself dissected. I am being pulled away. My soul is torn apart.

And you bend down, trying to gather the pieces. I see, but it is already less clear, like the beginning of my blindness. My vision is fragmented. I see only a part of you. Your face I see still; its sudden ghastly pallor. And your hair, the only red tincture that remains in my vision. You are vanishing, Henrietta, diminishing before me. You do not cry out. It is the silence that strikes me. You dissolve, my Duchess, you evaporate. The world of flesh is drawing away. There is nothing substantial remaining.

'Thence by a soft Transition, we repair
From earthly Vehicles to these of Air.'
Our love cannot be contained in wax, Henrietta. That is all I know.

e
nic laight

nic laight was born on the
23rd of april 1968.

A NIGHTMARE in reflexion. A vegehuman, breathing in the smell of an earth and alienode, born on a refuse-sight. Contamination spawns across un-charted cess-plains, and maggot stud-farms, lodging within tubes of broken and shredded trash, against pyramids of white worms, after supporting the morning sun upon poolpits of oily shit, atop abandoned corpses and the still dead strata. Worms fend off the carrion gulls.

By a consepticoupling he comes; by two black figurine twisters in a thick methane cloud; prepuce and labial tear coming-screams gripful of manelice and stinking tongues lilt all over in silhouettes to form a chilld. Labour ejects tumorous guts within gestatory time. The female host lies: flesh punctured by rusted bed springs, the bloodew went helter skelter round-andown. The wombug comes feet first into the world's rancid peelings. Its head remains womb-fast for the afternoon, leg stumps pelting welts upon its Mamahind. She attempts to rise against the pain, upon paws or suckers: pillars for her weight. Aghast, the being-born gains a safe footing, between the bones of a lard and pupae infested rib-cage, to struggle; twisting free each way, incalcified. The Mother pushes upon the head-swollen belly. Tiny feet, sharp nails, wriggle livid. Mother-hairs amongst hot embers, crackling fuses to the whitened scalp. Sensation: against the vagina, perineum and anus, white-hot cast iron faeces amass. The mother grins [out], grits [down], and shatters [away] her teeth (splinters exchanging gumholes) with Lilith in hand, wrighting the name, so consumed in blind and dental pain. She clutches the brood's (exo)-genitalia to dename it from the ovoid.

"Thee! Thee O! Thee O bDUD!"

Extensive-rip, revelation of her vertebrae. The white torso and limbs remain still as the head rocks about. It twists free to the sound of flatus and emptying plugholes.

Arise great blue head, below blood and mucus! Hail skull four times larger than the body forever!

It looks to the greengas horizon, stiff-necked and dour. In the comet-red light of the evening, ma-guts make a net of curls over his entire body; magusts wind around and feed upon the slimy scalp.

A halocloud rises above bDud, a mutation of black moths let free, followed by hungry bloat flies; winged lice with fist sized armour-spheres, rocketoads burping, slicing prey with razored tongues.

In that world, bDud's first infant cry scatters the gulls to the thermals. His second peal attracts the honeyed rats to his mother's yet tepid corpse. His third toll murders; upon the trash mounds, human scavengers faint into deep pools of rotting matter, asphyxiating on strings of rancid milk, semen, soft bags of brown-red colonic irrigative, and the pulped skin of blighted fruit. The elderly die this way.

Youth flee into the shantyre town to be attacked by the bred parasites in their nightmyres: incoherent scenes of apocalypse, acromegalic blue-brain channels, Theo bDud showing through, clambering across the offal towards them; a voyaging obscene frame, gnawing at its umbilical scentrope, chased by leaping rats fighting over the after-birth. The nightmares invariably lead to calm, thankful, suicides.

[How bDud leaves the dump, enters the town, and finds a home.]

Below a shanty roof, nine yet alive bare-bone cadavers, with saywoe eyes and buckled-buck teeth, crouch in shadowed sways, in their suffocating dwell. Picking at their lice, they, scales falling from their eyes, discern the cuckoo-bDud enter. He breathes ptomaine-halitotic death fumes into the seven children, piling their limp dead bodies, smallest first, into the larder. Its hollow walls contain the ghosts of a trillion ma-got lives. Bid and Tally Chthone smile weakly at their adoption. It evolves that bDud is partially self-nurtured to know, from the damp trapezoidal shreds of litype and newsprint, layereams from the belly to the breath of this dump, that it was black that begat bDud: that - out - of - the - nihil - blight - fire - black - begat - black - begat - grey - and - gray - begat - grave - begat - blank - and - begone - bore - belame - bDud - begone - a - gain - and - the - mother - was - MAPA: a naked line without children.

bDud: a blue head; a (reel away) gain; a malignant festering lewd weltbulb or abortumor; a reeking onionhead with winged black eyebrows in a proboscidean state; sockets full of worldweary darkness, and enpowdered porcinez and fatty rollback preputial necks. His butt is clean bar his coprophilial vacations; excrementitious sittings upon choice imported oriental faeces, placed atop the seat of a varnished three-legged stool-stool: the oriental black buds like coprakernels with quick dry surfaces and spreading centres; into his creamy onanus at bilious and smegmal re-past repasts [rpt]. He is yet another way of exclamation; an unspeakable being of fun-filth.

[The skin grown over the world's mouth]

The hairless head surfaces against the vast backdrop of the un(i)verse, leaving a sop-heavy lip upon the floor, where bacteria-ptyalin is feeding. His resurrected head is the bulk of a satellite. As vast an umbral head and face on the wasting line of the narrative horizon. Waiting by the shanty door for the eclipse, a shadow forms, racing across the phisog or milleniache: a grimace to see and smile upon the earth, with his mouth portraying a chicken anus, or human anus: being-lip-eczematous. Again a vast blue cephalicyst eclipses an unseen sun, and upon the dark side the final raylight beholds the human moan....

Theo bDud is a virtual aphonic muterror. His cracked lower lip drools hoary inexhales back and forth, blasting wheezy contamination. His tonguelet, at birth, was an obmutescent canker-nipple in a rotten mouthole. Nothing more can be said of it. Later, it is war-spoil stuffed with dental remoulds. It is a rank and golden sphinctoration below black eyes that eye the spills of blight upon the globe. At the reception of the dataworld, of its sunkentropic events, his teatongue trills ululous titters E E E E E E E E E E E . [The castraltongue frequency: beat of the gnatwing] This is a truly comic sounding.

Theo bDud and his living vocation is to shower death upon the globe. For what is Theofear, if not fragmeaning? He is a featherless bulk, hands deep, at pubis, in pockets or, extracted. His fat palm wets his lips to shaft and spittle-wax his eyebrows out and dampen his cracked scalp down, smarmcooing at the dead and dying. Shock-stock-taking what were just remains: lividity re-maimed.

Standing wide by the hot blue muzzle of a Howitzer field gun, flanked by gaunt irregulars (soiled artillery grunts with hand rolled fags, flaccid and infused to their dry lips), Theo bDud, silent within a black pinstripe, trills slightly, gurning at imploded roof slates and screaming limbless children; in europastoral towns, eastasian cities, islamarshes, plains, and vaalleys. In a turn towards the breach he nods: the pull of the firing cord, the damp palms over their ears:

BOOM B₀₀OOM

eeeeeeeeeeeeeeeeeeeeeeeeeeeeeeeeeeeeeeeeee

There is recoil. The path is through the trace; by the trajectory of speeding matters. And as he turns, pleased, from the paunch, he holds a soldier's gaze, trilling and glowering, raising his dyed brows and puckering his flaking anal lips. Again EEEEEeeeee! onionhead bDud exclaims, to the nervous gaze, coming across his own rare smile in a broken hand mirror [sniper-sighter] hung from the greasy neck of a nervous gaze.

Historicity: grim visaged hostilities and necrologic. The women, men, and children shrink from bDud's range as he enters the ArcsaSascrian war zones. As if his stench is more putrid and emetic than that of the bulldozed corpses driven along the main thorough-fare before his black field coach: a welcoming gesture of the local militia. The horses are blinded, nostrils corked. As he enters the town, dogs are silenced, fun-erals are postponed. Birds fly north in winter. Ani-mals sleep through the spring. As bDud enters a boar-droom in the town, the window-panes are willed to mist over. The walls willed to weep. A green haze, the stench of rotten fish, pervades the space. Attempts at taking notes in his company are useless. Ink is willed to freeze. Pages, by his will, turn sodden. Minds veer to images of... As he leaves the meeting, through thresholds, Theo bDud lowers his huge blue head. The grotesque tuber meets his swollen breasts and raised cockstandard. A copper bell on a spiral spring, set into the door's lintel, sounds dull against the shrill, exiting, "EEEEEeeeee!" It is difficult to ascertain his age. Some say it is a matter of centuries, others whisper a billieon behind him. Wagers are never taken. Probabilities are a will of bDud.

Is he a misshapened Venusian, mollusc, or ir-radiated coleoptera? Comments upon the mature T.O. bDud codex: a pixifoto of sepia shit, of homun-cles bDud: in the con-sense of a BuddhaPig, PapUbu,

Maefly West, and Martian Helldagger. His obesity doesn't seem to suggest excess flesh, fat, glands, or heavy bones. Instead it recalls a thin membrane resisting the innards (wet red tubes and black gristly organs, thick yellow bones and grey-green offal) awaiting the merest rent in the semolina hide.

bDud's awkwalk movements are not aided by caliper, crutch, or stick, but by naked, twin (uniovular) five-year-old girls (large grey eyes and thin lips); shivering white rests for bDud during his morning sessions. His elbows are supported by their upbraided heads of hair. Through a nasal effort, Theo bDud, in conjunction with well rehearsed hand m(e)assages, translaights his silencEEEeees into the twins' voices. By alternating nasal hum, short trill, and dual fingering of the girls' ear lobes, his meanings become shy chatterings.

[an examplea: red-rivet old man]

Theo bDud moves, incomplex-six-legged-permutations, across the dusty road to arrest, from the refugee-Q, an old man whose face is blanched with fear. "Come with me," bubble the giggles.

That is, an elderly man chosen by the jaw, above this broken Arcsas town, on a stretched lea-side. Naked, within his shot silk smoking jacket (a token from the recent dead), shot through with blooded stars, snipered holes in the shimmering cloth, he is

touched upon the sallow jowl by Theo's fetid pal-
ministry. Old man thin-king with very whey-white
skin: "Vaguely," he says, "always, they are having
enough rounds to put into flesh and bone, and always
there is a day, and a night, and nothing, then the putting of the tired and the miserable out of their day
life."

He is a living corpse of a sag, his scarlet rags open;
on his knees, staring at his genitals, dust scraping the
underside of his sac. Touching his temples to the left,
the muzzle of a gun; to the right a pick blade.

The old retired surgeon is happy to exit this way, really being-afraid of bDud today. The black flies, of
course, those black flies that remain with him for a
while upon the lea-side, buzz.

[red-rivet flies]

Missing narratives are soon inferred. Black Mayflies,
mating, are placed upon the geriatprick, right upon
the weary head, if you so call, and with the Theo's
rusty scissors around his dying-liver handspots, the
blades close once SNAP around the base of his prick.
SNAP!

A true, reported alternative: Theo bDud holds the
point of a knife to the eye of a retarded child, motion-
ing him to bite the old man's testicles off.

Geriatprick falls before pain can form; a second

snip of the sac, SNAP, and the mating flies and Theo dance... eeeeee.

[red-rivet refugee-Q]

...beside the avalanche warnings of blackened and bloated corpses falling, stopping the flow of refugees envectored by hunger and shells along the only road out of the town, their weak gait rising to the cratered summit, there to be met by a single bullet and sent falling by a boot up the arse, a bullet in the backspine, yet alive to sear, freefellscree down from the heights to crack their heads, broken melons, upon the road before the constant line, stopping the flow of refugees envectored by...

[a bDudian twin vocal possibility: red-rivet MaPa]

"Fuel the screaming. Die alone! That is their matter, the condemned, dying to tell all of their inevitable onticide, fucking uncontrollable flatus breath wide red fu✄✄✄✄✄ mouths and fu✄✄✄✄✄ smaller minds Ach! I'll just see to the fu✄✄✄✄✄ cunt-cock faced lot of them now, cunt or prick all arseholes of course! No discrimifu✄✄✄✄✄nation! I should've had a rule of silence your fu✄✄✄✄✄ lives or your fu✄✄✄✄✄ tongues, or I'll take the fu✄✄✄✄✄ lot of you out. Get this! like a bunch of tin crabs the other day pissing eyes on the end of their stalks, shuffling

e

side to side I made them fu⋊⋉⋊ whatever hot rods/
mincers/rusted taps/broken bottlenecks under the ig-
nited gas. Before the fair gloom of my chamber those
chilledren, with their ash-wode toys on string, trailing
in their PaMa's mudd and urime up the path to the
chamber. Little beings more concerned with the
woden sailing ship run aground on the mudflatus
than death: 'Oh, Oh maapaa, loook its got dirty,
maamee I want a pisshit?' And the parents! The
fu⋊⋉⋊⋉⋊⋉ parents even let them drop to their
haunches and do the f⋉c⋊⋉⋊⋉⋊ thing a f⋊⋉k-
⋊⋉⋊ pace away from ME? Well I will be their ven-
geance. The nuclear hue of their eyewhites in the
snufflounge comet trails in a dim concrete, asbestos,
and lead dissecting chamber by the artificial light
from the adjacent coils burning. A bright, luminal
scene. I prefer them alive, still standing at least, with
their eyeballs extracted, placed to tic-toc-roll against
their jowls, those cheeky videohs view of their naked
blackblue toes in chamber foot-rot It's a f⋉c⋊⋉⋊⋉⋊
glorious noise they make considering this terrible
acoustic de-sign. Severance of the wet optic-nerve. In
a turn, off with their lights!! EEEEEEeeeee Have all
the screams and pleas for me faded yet? It's all in the
right name right?! THE O bDUD. F⋊⋉K⋊⋉⋊ bDUD
by morn, F⋊⋉⋊⋉I⋊⋉⋊ bDUD at dusk. Multiply my
fucking name THE O bDUD in every fucking line,
place and time inbetween. Don't fucking mess with
these names. Just repeat the fucking thing, in the dark,

nic laight

after me THE O bDUD I am the Hero."

All exist ultimately at the mid-point between the twin
states of Arcsas and Sascra, upon the crimson Axcyst
bridge, above the river Cyst: a site for the war's official
closing ceremony; folly-ful bunting is arrayed across
the warm girders. Two deaf blast-bands (the ensem-
bles of muzzle-mouthpieced sidearm pipers, detun-
ing to a cut-up chorus of their respective civic an-
thems, with carbines and oil-soaked colts pressed to
their pursed lips; tooting through to the de-shelled
chambers) hearalding the bDudian field car's arrival; a
black bier-like autobile, with a handsome, finger-
stitched, human-hide upholstered crib for the dwar-
fish slime, bDud.

Interpretations through his trills: gathering here for
the closing ceremony they find him standing on the
brink. This is told. This is expected. This is performed
with an infantrite. An answer resides in the loud noise
of chaotic messages delivered to the bridged line of
victims, showered and naked.

SPLIT THE FUCKING CORPSES UP FROM
PERINEUM TO THE BABE'S MILKSNOT-
DROP!

Again his large blue head, a hellipsoid upon the red
bridge at sunset; almost the silhouette of his faint

178

scalpcilia. His veins sign-out for a Mariana trench or trace of an Atlantean mutant as seen from an ex-traterra cameramonitor circling an obscure marble-viewed earth. His photoputrid head is the babe of the world and a father to one and All, a friend to all of us on earth. His soft uncallused hands are upon the swathed child, no bigger than he, ripped away from its wetnurse. Her broad-nipple sliced off, forming a swete for its milksnotdrop mouth.

A series of babacoos for Theo before drowning: "AAAAAAeee BBBBBeee a Sadseed dying, hee heff gheenus, he hayte thee noyse." To this, bDud orders a booted stamp on the smooth and teething babe, and drops it into the River Cyst. The nipple lozenge falls free. This can never be understood, never seeing the fly in the hornet.

SPLIT THE FUCKING CORPSES UP FROM SENILE PERINEUM TO THE BABE'S MILKSNOTDROP... NOW!!!!

His sonic film voice never sounds exactly sane, but he calls for the finishing blows and the jaw bone spoils. The geistscreams bite and blow great gales at sea, gurning the waters to the riverbelow. These are phan-tom-childe induced storms, far above the dusky high-rise cirro-stratus.

It is Theo bDud's last chance to call once, to call the child born to call it drowning call it brilliant white then in its falling-turning, then call it away, too soon... told the evening read in dusklights, too soon. He says, calling to nothing, being only one, letting the blood-flow go to where the bridge ceases; he continues further, forward, will-be-blown.

[red-rivet red-rivet]

He counts red-rivets to follow his/tory: the effluvia of death. To continue; his ico-nic-nacs to fondle; spun on the bier's bonnet acting as a top, a spinning top, re-volving smoothly with a disturbing tin-hum. Around him the entire celebridge is a tally of his produce. He counts each rivet as a corpse. So many thousand red-rivets counted on an abacull; lives taken by bDud, not over a century or a year, but in month of work be-tween Arcsas and Sascra in the monument of the Ax-cyst Bridge. A rivet for an old man. Red-rivets for scalps. A rivet for each limblown child. Red-rivets for his Chthonic brothers and sisters. Rivets for scaven-gers. A rivet for every one in the refugee-Q. Rivets for bulldozed corpses. A red-rivet for MaPa.

Placed into his pocket compartment; he abandons his speeeeeeches, counts the columns, numbers the war zones-afar, remembers his childhid, and farts. This is noted by the river, upon this happy day, above the Cyst.

Oh! bDud kisses rot-red-rivets, above a riverbed; placing semispherics into his mouth. The fat-head of a

red-rivet into the fat head of Theo, passing back and
forth atop his clit-oral-bud, softly. Sooooft-ly. eeeeee.
Columns of rivets are counted eeeeeee by the river-
background.

Red-Rivets: pneumatic jabs of scarlet iron. These
cold reds were sent from Arcsas, the country place,
built November to January, by common sorts. De-
cember blows away, and while, in red, the red-rivet
counting and killing machine continues, endlessly,
and the sun seems far away. Here, Theo is riveted to
the de-naming; one side of the numbers recounting
stabler times.

[red-rivet scalping]

As bloody screams grow from the terrorised, trembl-
ing with fear, smellhead bDud Bluehead falls into the
scene from Dark Sky. bDud catches an escapee by the
fender-bump-her of that black field-car, by the cold
red-rivets. The wet scalp hangs down from her head,
attached to the nape of the neck. Hands and fingers
are broken, out of joint [probably tied to a bolder and
smashed with a small, round, yet heavy stone]. The
feet and pelvis similarly. There is evidence of torture.

[red-rivet disembowellment]

Head of the God of Number O. Heads twisted out of
joint smoulder, by the lit firewood tied to his back. A

nic laight

Captive. He felt little pain, from sternum groin he had been disembowelled. His head leans to one side. Error!! One is mistaken. His insides are at his feet. EEEEEEeeeeee!

[red-rivet jawlessness]

Theo's hand strokes a chin in a ceremonious mime. The act, now in preparation, is for the removal of the jaw from its living owner. The old trickery of bDud. Be not mistaken, the victims do attempt to shout something, or at least try to speak. Bound, panting for life, jawless, fingers are broken in a deft act. The tongues remain out, lolling against the chests, dog-like. The broken hands grip and tear; with their last energies they attempt to replace their tongues. Theo bDud places the jaw of a gibbon into broken hands. Their heads lean to one side.
CHIN. JABBER. SIMIAN. JUT.
Again, one is mistaken, their insides are at their feet eeeeeeee.

[red-rivet: muzzle-velocity of flyblow enema]

Placing a pound of black maggots into a funnel, and filling it with warm water, an enema is forced upon an unshaven, naked man. The flyblow feed upon his internals. Once upon the Axcyst Bridge, he is taken out of the rectal constraints only to fall to his face and

182

knees. A stirring black string of pellets explode from his rear. With each pop, a single bluebottle exits and buzzes free. The air is filled with a burning fragrance as the host burst. At once, fallen man becames the dispersing pixel-ebon cloud.

[The Case of The O bDud Dissembling]

In the river-bed, the watered ditch below, are the findings of the past. bDud, at the bridge-fort, calls commands; catalogues, to execute by ceremony in the morning lifting and turning the chins of the walking in the red-fall smelling the rivets in the ocean.

He is not in Sascra or Arcsas, the civic places. He remembers; there are real acts, true decimations, that I will never repeat. The water is the paving to other doors, his black-wash to the bridge; kissing the rivets, counting and accumulating. Evening slams, so white goesto the rest of the light-left.

Ten Billion rivetsymbols remain, the production being exported. Theo wets a hot one, hissing; then baptised in black. The smirk rolls at the world; the Arcsas-Sascra turmoil isn't over. So eight lives a minute never have a meaning. The joke, in his smirk, widens; seven seconds remain. Not long. Boat not far. A change in the mode-land of our abodes. Go west, he says, with rivets in pocket, lost, going east, meeting at six. Far back, the autobier fell into the river. He thinks much of his rivets.

Theo bDud places a hand into his pocket, for a rivet [the placing of his wet palm around a jaw]; all or nothing, for the red-rivet call, and he jokes with the river, its flow, and what is remaining and what is reaching up-river. Two seconds remain. The boat is near. Being alone is such a funny thing, without a chance of your memory enduring. Never as long as things are left to erase: note the need to continue, going on and on. For the profitable Industry of the RedRivet. He is in Riveted eternity.

At dusk. A camera-shutter blinks. The excentricity of the red bridge is revealed. Reason darkens. Unseen objects are, in a way. Upon the side of a globe, there now, near darkness, facing out, is a vile sight, at times misted by darkness, at other times fogged. By a light, placed beneath the water, a bDud appears ghastly, underlit. A bDud-figure wills a way on a last day fallen. Then Axcyst bridge appears serene, isolated from what is upon a globe's surface. Several slow over-passes show a girdered and suspensory pontoon, through skeletal beams into a ritual space. Coming in low, a red bridge is no more than a frame or shelf. Again, partially roofed. Again, no more a shelter than bare boughs in an orchard or a courtyard. The shelf contains a figure, a bDud-like figure, a dark mist, a light fog, and All that has being upon a globe's surface. Or, seen stock still-framed, a globeless shelter: a bDud-figure placed upon a white or black backing. By a remark Theo re-reads at least, outwards, prone, from one aspect of a globe, lightless, facing away, an utterance about his character, saying, that is: at times, I really am the Truth.

As the sun falls upon Axcyst Bridge, and the rivets are counted and the blood is broomed away with salt, lime, and freshwater, Theo bDud stands upon his stoolstool and puts his paunch upon the guardrail. Opening his arms above the twins, he sniffs the black smoke carried from a steam whistle over the still, scarlet waters. A practised spit turns into a feeble dribble, strung onto the deck of the passing boat at curtain call. To those who read him well, receive this:

WELCOME YOU FUCKING FOOLS / GLAD TO HAVE YOU WITH ME AGAIN.

Now below the bridge, a beaded curtain of entrails swings and glistens in the last breeze. Now clearing the low marsh haze, out of the purple grown deltoid horizon, the obsidian mast of a shallow bowed boat slides up-river. It rears in minute increments. Atop the wide and low schooner, the poly-figurative crew sway about the crow's nest: a multi-limbed Shivaring Beast. Simultaneously, a jabbering bouquet of mariners. Spyglass to each eye every 45degrees; these anteaural searchwrights are deemed frenetic to watch, from a distance, by the ganeshing Theo bDud.

nic laight

The rigging is cat's cradled from the mast. The ship is one week out of Sascra, after picking up 63 idiots of the Guerilla Paniclan (now below, within the hold, ratshit, rats, and shit to their shins). Two days in, one of the older women [a synchrofanatic] began a rhythmic chant above the general bombilation. From deep within, without ceasing her lululululululululululu lululululululululululululululululululululululululululululu lululululululululululululululululululululululululululululu lululululululululululululululululululululululululululululu lululululululululululululululululululululululululululululu lululululululululululululululululululululululululululululu lululululululululululululululululululululululululululululu tonecycle for breath, she pisses air by gullet spasms. Hour to hour the piercing corrugated tone persuads sympathetic re-calls amongst the missing 62. The hull begins to shiver and sets up tidal bores to the river-bank.

Airwaves, moved, flow into Theo bDud upon the bridge. It may sound like laughter in their chanting, but there is no hilarity. Hear? It is merely the aural illusion of the tone:
A shrill, nauseating, paronomasia.

triptych

david charles harold

david harold gave up writing
at the age of nineteen for a
life of adventure, first in the
dutch army, then eventually
finding himself in aden and
harar where he smuggled
guns, coffee, and slaves. a
close friend of the poet
verlaine, he left behind only
a small body of work on his
premature death in 1891. a
lifelong catholic, born under
the sign of cancer with
cancer rising, david harold
was a genius, inspired to
greatness by the mysterious
trinity of the tenth of
november. the fragments of
his writing remaining are
treasured classics and he is
sorely missed.

I

SHE DIDN'T wear a seat-belt. If we'd crashed she'd have gone flying through the windscreen. I wore a belt and would have watched as she hit the road: tiny shards of glass freckling her skin, jagged branches of bone sprouting from her flesh.

Thinking of how these thoughts excited me, a nausea, as insistent as any erection, sits in my stomach.

We had frequent accidents: bumping fenders, sliding across the roads, running curbs. We ricocheted through the city.

"I believe every time should be like walking through fire without getting burnt," she said. She was talking about fucking. I gripped the leather seat, suffused with a tremendous energy I'd rarely known before.

She smiled as she looked at me. She didn't know

david charles harold

what I was thinking: she could die in the space of that smile. The freeways are treacherous at night.

She was opium: languid, but always on the edge of some passion or danger. Occasionally she'd hold my hand as we flew down the roads. I felt something. I imagined love buried in her womb, instead of the coil, that bone that made her safe. I thought of her as a needle, a tiny metal reed that transfused blood and strange chemistry.

In bed, the lines of her body, taut, were offered. I submerged them in my hold, entering into her. Minor adjustments of knees and chins locked us together, the geometries of our bodies like an origami sculpture.

Afterwards we lay in the delicate surrender forbidden by our distrustful worlds. I wondered, even in those early days, how long we could survive like that; living on sin and skin. It was all so fragile and I had no sense of grace. What little I have now I learned from her.

There was a song she liked to hear on the radio in the car that went: "You break my heart in two / That's a piece for me and a peace for you." Back then it was just something she liked. Thinking about it now, I realise how much I love this hurt: the knowledge of love and its futility.

In the car she said: "You are fucking Her. You were seen holding hands."

And: "We consecrate the virtue of murdering the

human heart."

And: "You won't say it? You'll just let me decide the truth?"

And: "I hate you."

And: "You feel you deserve nothing, but you never get what you deserve."

And: "Let's stop."

And: "I hate you."

"I have drowned in the fountain of you," she said.

I told her real people don't talk like that. But I ached. Once I used to believe the most unlikely things. Then I met her and they were all true. I wished I could be inside her, there in the car, make love to her with all the certainty that possesses the act. But I couldn't, and I doubted.

Parked in the car she said: "I had another dream last night. I remember... me sitting cross-legged. You were inside me, trying to get out. I had to hold you in, even though you were scratching my insides. My mother was there, telling me I was pregnant. I am late. She kept insisting. Later, I was in a restaurant. It was called Palomino Lux, which I can link back to an article I read the other day and, well, fuck that. It was another dream about Her, okay? I dreamt that I stole Her coat, which was long and red. I was going to steal a bag of narcotics out of Her pocket, but I put the coat back instead. I don't remember if you were still inside me. Jesus, why do I keep dreaming about Her? I hate you. I never knew the touching you."

II

One day things were transformed.

I woke up and found I'd turned into a bug. I was the last human on a planet devoid of life. I discovered that the world I thought I knew was actually an alien zoo and we were all just exhibits. I don't know. Things were just transformed.

I sat and stared at her, thinking about how alien her shape seemed under the sheets. I remember best the exquisite patina of semen, dirt and blood that covered my hands. The lace of love. I scratched at it as I wondered what I was. She shook a little as she slept.

Eventually she woke.

"I'm sore," she said.

"Oh," I said.

"I'm going to leave you."

"Right. Would you like anything?"

"No," she replied. "Not really."

"Okay."

She stood. "Strange eyes," she said. She came to me then and I couldn't resist holding her, my hands smoothing up from her waist, resting on her shoulder blades.

"Wings," I said. Up close she felt so different. So much less alien. Perhaps with this flesh I could....

"I'm going," she said.

There are points beyond which some changes cannot be made.

But when she'd gone, I discovered she'd left her coat. The wind rocked the glass in the cradle of its frame, and I watched the raindrops shiver, momentarily pausing in their races down the window. How could she have been so careless of the weather, I thought. I went after her. I expected her to be on her way to her car. Instead, she was sitting on the bench in the courtyard of my apartment building. Her make-up had run, making her face look like it had been smeared with ash.

I sat beside her, trying to still her shaking.

"Don't," she said, "I like being cold. It reminds me I'm alive."

She told me another dream:

"I see Her apartment. It's spartan and white. The only real detail I can remember is a David Bowie poster over the bed. She comes home from somewhere. I don't know where, but She's been gone a long time. Her phone is ringing. I watch Her talk to someone on the phone. I don't remember. Then you arrive and don't speak. Just lie down with Her on the floor and start to go down on Her. Or you fuck Her. I don't want to watch but I have to. Because I want to see if you hurt Her like you hurt me. I want to see if you rip Her and bite Her and fuck Her in the ass. But you don't. Someone else is there too and you make them watch or join in. Then I wake."

Finally she let me hold her. I tried to squeeze the

dream out of her as we sat with rain-water in our eyes.

"We're so clever at being sick aren't we?" she said. "So ill."

As time went on I didn't know whether to kiss her or kill her, and I think, to her, those options didn't seem so far apart. We had come together thinking we'd sate the hunger we felt. But we had fed off each other. Now we were husks, tatters of muscle and protrusions of rib. In retrospect, perhaps one morsel remained that we could have relished—the heart—but we were too busy devouring the flesh to differentiate.

The last time I heard her voice before I left was on my answering machine. I had just returned from the station.

"Apparently we can both be cured," she said.

But I'd already bought my ticket.

There was a new city, but it was full of ghosts. They paraded across my bed, each more like her than the last. Perhaps I was forgetting how she really was.

III

We were talking about true love. I wasn't much part of the conversation. Lent had come and gone and I'd given up everything, packing up my wrinkled shirts and a box of books that weren't mine. How she found me again was anyone's guess.

"Magic," she said. "The first law of magic is that a magician is only as strong as her desire. But with a strong enough desire everything else is secondary—the ritual, the incantations, belief even. Wanting is the secret of magic."

"I saw you in my heart," she said.

Across the street a woman in a Chanel styled plaid suit took a snapshot of the diner. What would she see later on her little square of paper? A young couple in grey and brown sitting behind empty coffee cups, finger tips not quite reaching each other across a formica table top. Or just tiny figures under a sign: OPEN 24 HRS A DAY.

Later we raged about love. She is beautiful I thought, all the time consumed by the need to flee. She looked like a black and white photograph, only blurred around the eyes where she had been crying. I had kissed those eyes. Slowly. Softly.

It was an old game, this rage, but the rules had changed forever, when I'd broken my vow of vigilance; sneaking out of the city on a night train. Tonight we would play to a different end—no collapse onto an unmade bed, to unmake flesh and forgive. Tonight she would not clench and hold tight, stirring me; still hard but tender inside her. She would not whisper that the language of love is speaking in tongues.

"Where once I saw things in black and white," she

said, "now, like me, they're black and blue."

"How can you expect me to get you through the night," I said. "I'm tired too. Your falling terrifies me."

"If I scare you into faith," she said, "I might just scare myself out of love."

"Faith in the faithless," I said. "I wish I could sew you shut and blind your eyes."

If we had seen ourselves in a movie in some too warm down town cinema with only seven dollar tickets at stake, we'd have walked out in disgust. We were crafting our lines and crafting them badly. When we should have walked away we stayed, secretly hoping to find a way to win against the other. We had turned love into war. Love's little ironies.

But there was a moment, when sudden headlights burned into the room like signs of warning, that I saw her again; the light on her skin that seemed to come from within, the killing detail of her dark eyes. And I wondered if the prize in this war wasn't love. I tried then to make my hand reach out and touch, but the weight of our individual furies had become more terrifying than that of an ocean.

"I'm drowning," she said. "Here in this tenement, in a city I'd never seen before today, I'm drowning."

We were feeling the same things, thinking the same thoughts, but could not connect in anything other than our dismay and bewildered loss. There was no place we could touch where we would not be pressing on a bruise.

When she finally fell asleep, still fully dressed,
curled like a question mark on my bed, I sat and
watched her breathing form. She still shook unexpec-
tedly as she slept, brief tremors that travelled her
length, then subsided again beneath her skin. She was
unquiet. At four she sobbed, for no longer than it
took me to smoke a dispassionate cigarette, but I
knew she was still sleeping. I tipped tiny periods of
ash into a white cup, punctuating my vigil. Flakes of
white stuck on the lipstick gummed rim of the cup,
and I allowed my attention to drift from my lover—
yes, still my lover—to a fragment like a snowflake, and
remain there until she stirred awake.

As she applied fresh make-up in the flat plane of my
shaving mirror, my vision expanded a little to take in
the red stain on the cup and I began to work on the
day's dialogue. Preparing my lines. I traced out the
shapes of the most obvious cruelties across the day,
drawn red, like the work of a lover's razor or the
smear of lipstick on a cup, a tissue, a cigarette. And
seeing that lipstick in my mind, seeing all the places it
touched on and around me, I missed her a little.

At my touch she flew.
"Fuck you! Why now? Why now?" she screamed.
"You deserve to fucking die!"
Ash rained on the room like a memorial and a bro-
ken cup lay by the wall: a jagged accusation.
We write love. Love is all metaphor. Love goes bad

and we stop writing and become written. But still. I felt something while she was there. It was only a moment but I felt it on my palms and it persists now, a ghost under my fingertips.

If she hadn't left then, I would never have had the strength to leave her a second time. It's not much of an ending I know but what can I say? I don't know myself, not really.

But she left and life returned to its parade of inconsequential details, of muttered ineloquence, hope only in sleep. I turned on the radio. Rocky Erickson was singing "if you have ghosts then you have everything." It's not much and it's not mine but it's the best explanation I have.

I sit in my room in an inch of ash and start to work magic.

For Jennifer Lyn Peet 1971-1991

fantastic ella macleod

matthew singh−toor

matthew singh-toor, the
son of an indian father
and an english mother,
was born near leicester in
1967. since his first degree
he has travelled and worked
in india, co-founded a
national group for people of
mixed racial heritage, and
taken a masters degree in
creative writing at the
university of east anglia. he
is currently working on a
collection of short stories
and a screenplay.

WE SIT IN THE GARDEN, under the banyan tree, and press jewels to our faces. I find an emerald, for Ella Macleod's eyes. She finds an amethyst, for my lips. I picture our flesh, glassy and smooth, shining upon the world.

A waiter, in faded maroon uniform and turban, stands at a distance, in the doorway of the hotel, half in shadow. He watches us, granite-faced. We must appear ridiculous, with our spangled faces.

Ella Macleod sifts through the jewels on the cane table-top. They click and slide. She makes her next selection and leans close, to dot tiny pebbles of onyx along my eyebrows. The tips of her fingers brush against the nap, and dislodge sun-bleached hairs from my cracked skin. They fall amongst the jewels on the table, and are lost in their light. I swallow, and choose to ignore this.

If truth be told, we have witnessed our own decay

matthew singh-toor

here. Over the weeks, Ella Macleod has watched the pigment flake grey from my face, the iris blanch milky in my eye. I am parched, twisted, frayed, like old rope. Ella Macleod's breath stings my eyeballs, buffets the bristles in my sore ears. But I deny this; always looking askance; always determined upon the fantasy:

We shine and move supple. The air is soft and gives to us. The earth cherishes our footsteps. We are at ease.

I press a ruby to Ella Macleod's forehead, like a bindi. The waiter disappears inside the hotel. I smile and wonder what he thinks of us.

The garden is screened by palms and cedars and mango trees; their trunks tangled together by shrubs and thorns. The smoggy, humid sky bulges down over a wide, patchy lawn, which is watered daily, haphazardly, by a rusty old sprinkler.

We have been sitting under the hundred-trunked, hundred-year-old banyan tree all day, every day, for months; drinking rose sherbet or tea. The centre-piece of the garden, it pushes its canopy wide up against the sagging clouds, and dangles scores of roots to the ground, like ropes. During the monsoon, they will slurp at the soil and, once established, once asserted, begin to thicken into new trunks.

The garden is always still and deserted, the hotel always empty. But if anyone did come, we could simply

202

climb up, and join the monkeys and crows in the branches above.

I know that Ella Macleod is humouring me; that I have pulled her unwilling into the garden. I know that we cast no light on the world; that the world casts light at us. I know that we are drying out, boxing in. But I hope she will not destroy the illusion today.

Ella Macleod tires of the jewels, and pours a cup of tea from the silver pot. I am soothed by the splash and gurgle, clean against the still air. Like a child, I demand, "Tell me the story again." The waiter, inside the hotel, hears me and comes to the doorway. He looks over at us, worried. Ella Macleod frowns slightly and, her Glaswegian voice a drone, begins:

"Once you provided a service.

"You sat all day in a white cubicle in a white office under a white light. On your white desk was a white pen, a white pad, a white computer, and a white telephone.

"You could mark black ink onto the white pad with the white nib of the white pen and you could mark green light onto the screen of the white computer by tapping the white keys on its white keyboard. These were the marks you were permitted to make.

"Your skin was brown and colour-full. But it did not shine under the white light. It felt like a stain and you were always waiting for someone to notice that it wasn't permitted.

"Beneath your skin bile rumbled green, pus ran yellow, blood rushed red.

"You had a recurring nightmare in which you punctured your finger with the white pen and spurted the bile, blood and pus all around the white office. The nightmare kept your flesh tense and made you wary of sharp objects. You were always prepared to cringe and flinch.

"The white telephone would trill at you. You were required to answer it, to listen to complaints, to mark characters onto the white pad and the white computer, to make appointments, to resolve problems, to reassure the plaintiff. Your voice felt like a stain on the air and you were ashamed to speak but as soon as you hung up the white telephone would ring again and you were required to answer it. High up on the white office wall was a white board which displayed the number of calls waiting.

"There were other white cubicles in the white office but you never looked inside them and you never spoke to their occupants. You could hear them though, chattering white noise down the white phones and between the white cubicles.

"You thought you were a filthy mark spreading insidious, repulsive over the white cubicle when really you were fading away. You didn't suspect that the white light rained down bleach.

"Until I called."

Ella Macleod understands me. She expresses my feelings. I could never explain how it felt to work in that office, but Ella Macleod describes it to a T. She is a godsend.

Her lips part as she raises her tea-cup, and I imagine the light streaming from her diamond teeth. Her jaw might be sculpted from rose quartz. I notice a piece blushing up from the table and, smiling, lazy, content, I hold it to Ella Macleod's face. She replaces her teacup and turns away. I know that she is tired of me. And I am afraid of what she might say.

I look over to the waiter. He is shadowy in the doorway, faded and framed, watching us, as usual. His hair is speckled grey and his maroon jacket is dusty with lime from the hotel walls. There are gold buttons missing from the jacket's front and cuffs.

I imagine the hotel's façade crumbling onto him; tired stucco and marble disintegrating, trickling into his hair, onto his uniform. Radiant in my cane chair, assured of my place in the world, I could smirk at this decay. I could laugh at him and call, "This will happen to everyone, except Ella Macleod and I!"

He walks across the lawn to us, and tidies the table-top. I fidget and look away. I know what his face is too delicate to say; that I am deluded; that I am stark staring mad. And I know that Ella Macleod's face says nothing to contradict this. So I refuse to look at either of them.

When the waiter is back in the doorway, I turn to Ella Macleod and ask, "Will you say what happened when you called me?"

She sighs, then nods slightly, and I know that her patience is near its end. This will be the last time she tells the story:

"You picked up the receiver expecting the usual white noise but instead my manic, skittish voice came giggling at you down the phone. I said:

'About bloody time excuse my language I've been holding on for twenty minutes literally twenty minutes with that recording telling me my call will be answered shortly I mean I think that's rude do you not to leave a person holding so long because I might have better things to do I mean this isn't the first time I've had to call no it's the seventh time yes the seventh time and still I've got no service I mean I'm sitting here like a big dummy and the service doesn't work and I don't think it's unreasonable to expect the service to work when I'm paying an arm and a leg for it I mean I know I'm just a name on the computer to you and I know that's not your fault because I'm sure they treat you like shite too excuse my language so don't get me wrong I'm not giving you a hard time I mean I'm sure you're sitting in some poky little office getting paid nothing for your trouble and bad working conditions etcetera because I've done that

kind of job myself and I know you must get sick
of taking abuse but I've got to talk to
somebody and it's better for me to exercise my
rights than to sit here with no service I mean we're
both being done over do you not think because in the end I know if I wasn't just a voice down
the telephone you'd understand and you'd want to
help me get the service back but they treat us
both like shite excuse my language so we both
get fed up and I take it out on you and you couldn't
care less and in the end they don't spare us a
thought when they're off enjoying themselves with their fancy things and they're
out laughing with their friends and we
just skulk about in the background and we're
always lonely and unnoticed I mean
they're the ones who have a place in the
world and they're easy in it and they're
comfortable and in the end it's their world
because they're the ones who feel at home
do you not think so will you not help
me?'

"You loved it. You loved what I said. You invested
what I said with significance. Other people would cut
me off as soon as they recognised my voice but you
would listen to me for hours. I phoned all the time
after that and always asked for you.

"I was ridiculed and condemned in white chatter

between the white cubicles. And you were noted as strange for your patience and sympathy with me when there were so many calls waiting."

Ella Macleod yawns and closes her eyes. I am anxious; she has changed the story. I whine, "What you said *was* significant, I didn't *invest it with* significance."

She ignores me and curls up on her chair. Over in the doorway, the waiter shakes his head slowly, from side to side. His turban is coming loose. If he does not rearrange it soon, the whole thing will unravel and fall to the ground.

"And why did you stop? You still have to tell me about the memo and our escape."

Ella Macleod pretends to be asleep.

I have not been paying attention; the garden has changed. The palms and cedars and mango trees are thinning out, shedding their needles and leaves. I thought they were evergreens. The shrubs and thorns are drying up, the grass is turning brown. Before long the garden will have no screen at all and the world will close back in on us.

I look up into the branches of the banyan tree, to console myself.

It grew from nothing into a trunk, which spread branches, which dropped roots from the air to claim the earth again and again and again, for hundreds of years, until there were hundreds of trunks.

*The monkeys and crows are at ease in it. The rest of the garden
bows to it; worships it. It keeps us.*

A sapphire catches my eye as it slips from Ella Macleod's face to the ground. I avert my gaze, but still
imagine the tumbling, flashing shards of amber and
opal and topaz which follow. Then I brace myself and
shake Ella Macleod awake, before it is too late. I
shout, "Tell me the rest! Tell me the rest now!"
    The waiter looks at his boots. He must be ashamed
of me. Ella Macleod stares hard into my eyes and spits
out the words:

"A white memo arrived on the white desk. It said:

TO ALL REPRESENTATIVES
RE: ELLA MACLEOD

It has come to our attention that one of our subscrib-
ers, a Miss Ella Macleod, has been making nuisance
calls to our Service Department. As our Service Representatives will be aware, Miss Macleod is dissatisfied
with the service she has received since becoming a
subscriber, and phones regularly to air her grie-
vances, many of which are quite unreasonable and
incoherent.

Over the past month, a series of obscene phone calls
has been made to our Freephone Sales number. The

calls have come from a woman, and been directed at our Sales Representatives. With the help of the Metropolitan Police, we have ascertained that the calls come from Miss Macleod's flat.

We have indicated to the caller that we have evidence of her identity and address, and we are now deciding whether or not to pursue the matter further. In the meantime, please refer any calls from Miss Macleod upstairs.

"You screwed up the white memo and threw it into a white bin. There was a hissing and a murmuring from the other cubicles; white whispered disgust:
    " 'Bitch... psycho... loser...'
"You clenched your fist and your fingernails gouged red crescents in the palm of your hand. Your flesh was ghostly in the white light. You stared at the white telephone till your eyeballs felt ready to burst, and you ignored its trilling. This was not permitted.
    "I still carried on calling the Freephone number after they told me they knew who I was. But eventually it was disconnected, and I just sat in my flat and waited for the police to..."

I bang my fist on the table-top and the jewels jump and clatter. Ella Macleod has distorted everything. The garden is warped before my eyes.
    "No!" I wail, "We escaped! I set fire to the memo and

yanked the phone out its socket. The alarm went off and the sprinklers blew up the computer. I kicked over the cubicles and ran out the office. I flew down the street and rammed my fist through a jeweller's window. I grabbed armfuls of diamonds and rubies and emeralds and sapphires and found you waiting in your flat. We took taxis and aeroplanes and flew here, to the garden, to shine upon the world together, to rest easy..."

I am crying. I am hoarse. The sun has cut through the smog, to crack open my head, burn my brain white. The jewels pour from Ella Macleod's face, and scatter on the table. She sweeps them to the ground with the side of her crumbling arm, and casts me a look of such fury, such contempt:

"No you stupid fucker you pathetic limp dick you don't know what you're talking about you never fucking well left your poky little office you just carried right on and answered the fucking phone you sat there like an arsehole and listened to them lie about me and the last thing you heard I'd been charged and locked up you cunt you useless pile of shite it was none of your fucking business you never even saw my fucking face you don't know anything about me you don't even fucking well know what I look like."

All the jewels are gone from Ella Macleod's face and she is right; there is nothing there but blank space. But her words have lopped the top off the world, and the annihilating light is flooding in.

The palms and cedars and mango trees rain down needles and leaves; swirling, fading, in a silent white wind. I wish that I could have stayed; I wish that Ella Macleod could have given me a little longer. But I have stopped fighting. I have stopped lying. I know that I stand no chance.

Over in the doorway, the waiter is up to his waist in crumbled stucco and marble. Through the wind and the light I make out his hand, waving, and hear him call, "Stark staring mad, you are stark staring mad." His image fades and the garden burns away to whiteness; the lawn flaring up last.

I climb up into the banyan tree and join the monkeys and crows. Wrapped around a bough, I am asserted, in fantasy, amid its hundreds of years. I press my ashen cheek against the bark and imagine it shining upon the world. Then I close my eyes, and prepare to awake, back in the white office, back under the bleaching light.